STARFELL

Willow Moss and
the Magic Thief

Books by Dominique Valente

STARFELL: WILLOW MOSS AND THE LOST DAY

STARFELL: WILLOW MOSS AND THE FORGOTTEN TALE

STARFELL: WILLOW MOSS AND THE VANISHED KINGDOM

STARFELL: WILLOW MOSS AND THE MAGIC THIEF

STARFELL

Willow Moss and the Magic Thief

DOMINIQUE VALENTE

ILLUSTRATED BY SARAH WARBURTON

HarperCollins *Children's Books*

First published in the United Kingdom by
HarperCollins *Children's Books* in 2022
HarperCollins *Children's Books* is a division of HarperCollins*Publishers* Ltd
1 London Bridge Street
London SE1 9GF

www.harpercollins.co.uk

HarperCollins*Publishers*
1st Floor, Watermarque Building, Ringsend Road
Dublin 4, Ireland

1

Text copyright © Dominique Valente 2022
Illustrations copyright © Sarah Warburton 2022
Cover illustrations copyright © Sarah Warburton 2022
Cover design copyright © HarperCollins*Publishers* Ltd 2022
All rights reserved

HARDBACK ISBN 978–0–00–830851–3
SPECIAL EDITION ISBN 978–0–00–854656–4

Dominique Valente and Sarah Warburton assert the moral right
to be identified as the author and illustrator of the work respectively.

A CIP catalogue record for this title is available from the British Library.

Typeset in Aldus LT Std 12/18pt by Sorrel Packham

Printed and bound in the UK using 100% renewable electricity
at CPI Group (UK) Ltd

MIX
Paper from
responsible sources
FSC
www.fsc.org **FSC™ C007454**

This book is produced from independently certified FSC™ paper
to ensure responsible forest management.
Find out more about HarperCollins and the environment at
www.harpercollins.co.uk/green

For Fudge, darling dog and dear friend

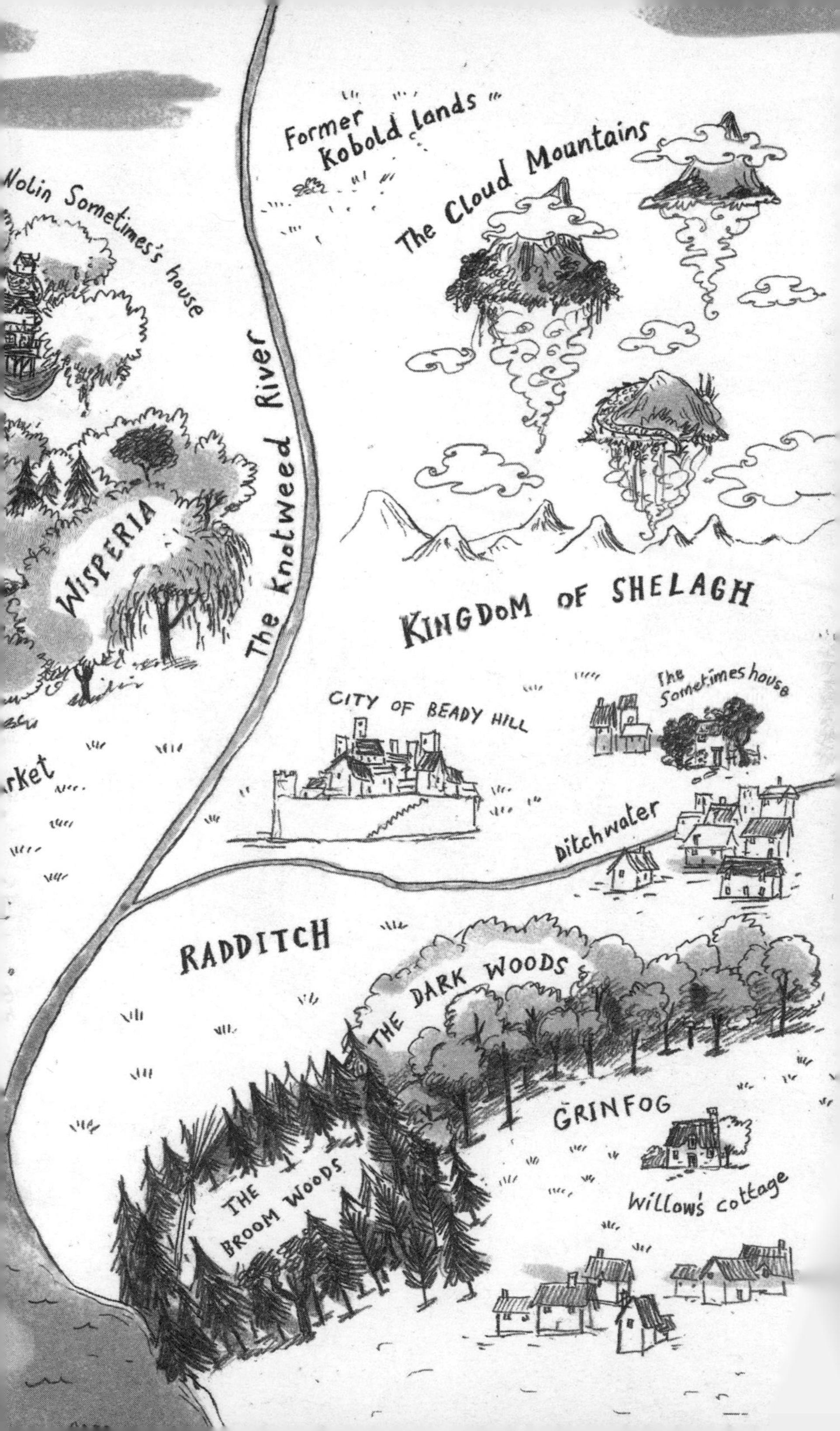
Former Kobold lands
The Cloud Mountains
Nolin Sometimes's house
The Knotweed River
WISPERIA
KINGDOM OF SHELAGH
CITY OF BEADY HILL
The Sometimes house
rket
Ditchwater
RADDITCH
THE DARK WOODS
GRINFOG
THE BROOM WOODS
Willow's cottage

1

Stolen Magic

The forest awoke like an old man with creaking knees, reluctant to start the day. There was a phlegmy sort of sound as if it were clearing its throat. Then it rolled its boughed shoulders and finally let the pink dawn trickle through the canopy with a grunt.

The soft light fell on to Willow Moss as she walked in the undergrowth, picking bark berries still coated with dew.

It was not yet spring, and winter was still hanging on by a fist – though it was possible to see the first signs of loosening fingers, like now, with the early berries. She popped one into her mouth. Tart yet sweet. Delicious. For just a moment, she could almost *forget* that her magic had been stolen, and that Starfell balanced on the knife-edge of war.

In the pale sunshine, with her basket full of the promise of spring, she felt almost normal – like an ordinary thirteen-year-old girl, alone in the forest, instead of one who'd been carrying the weight of everything that might go wrong on her small shoulders.

Until recently, Willow had been a young witch with the magical ability to find lost things. In fact, she had developed the reverse side of her power too: the ability to make things disappear.

It was just over a month ago that the dangerous wizard Silas had got his hands on a powerful old elvish staff and used it to steal her magic.

Willow had fought him as hard as she could, holding on to the staff even as he'd used it to drain her powers. She had only let go when the very part of the staff that allowed it to steal magic – shaped like an iron half-moon – had torn free. Using the very last drops of her ability, Willow had managed to make it disappear from the staff and reappear in her hand.

Shortly afterwards, Silas had been captured and imprisoned in the Cloud Mountains by the rock dragons. This, as far as anyone knew, was where he remained. But, by stealing Willow's powers, including the one that allowed her to disappear, he could work

out how to escape at any moment. And, if he did, there was one thing everyone was sure of: he would be coming for *Willow* – and the missing piece of the elf staff that would allow him to steal magic.

Automatically, Willow's hand reached inside her pocket and traced the edges of the iron half-moon.

She pulled it out and watched as it glittered gold in the low light. It hadn't glittered before – the sparkle was thanks to a rare and powerful substance known as wispdust, which she'd sprinkled on the piece of metal to protect it from being discovered by magic. Moreg Vaine had shown up at her door with the glittery powder not long after Silas was captured. Willow, too, drank a daily tonic containing wispdust, so Silas could not use magic to find her either, if he came back.

Willow kept the iron half-moon with her always, even in her sleep. She was ready to defend it with her life. The only thing that had made the loss of her magic almost bearable was the fact that, without this missing piece of the staff, Silas wouldn't be able to steal anyone else's abilities . . .

Unless he found another way. And she was sure he would stop at nothing to rip the magic out of Starfell for himself.

Something Granny Flossy had once told her drifted into Willow's mind: *'The thing about worry, child, is that there's the good kind and the bad kind. The good kind is like an animal pricking up an ear to listen to something rustling in the grass. The bad kind is when we give it so much of ourselves that we forget to live, and forget to rest, so that when the rustle arrives we're too tired to actually do anything about it.'*

Willow had definitely been doing too much of the bad kind of worrying, listening for phantom rustles in the dark.

She put her hairy green carpetbag on the ground, close to a clump of spotted purple mushrooms, and ate some more berries, watching the forest come to life.

A fife tree stretched as it awoke, and Willow noticed that it was dotted with strange black spots all along its bark. It shivered, almost like it had a cold. Before she could wonder about that, though, a small hairy creature with a very large beard, known as an elth, darted between the tree's roots, a pile of currant buns in his wrinkly dun-coloured hands.

Willow watched him go in surprise. She'd never seen one up close. She was probably staring too hard because he stopped and made a rude gesture at her, which was elthish for 'bog off'.

Not knowing this, she waved. There was a tiny squeak, followed by a tiny eye-roll.

'Daft beggar. That big'un got another fink comin' if it reckons it's getting its monster mitts on me mam's fresh buns.' Then he dashed away.

Willow snorted, stifling a mad impulse to pinch one of the buns just to see the look on his leathery face. Soon afterwards, a soft plume of steam floated up from the mound below, and

Willow figured he must be putting the kettle on for tea.

She opened up the carpetbag to check on Oswin, the monster from under the bed and her best friend. He was a species of monster called a kobold, but asleep he looked even more like a cat than usual. His eyelids flickered when she lifted one of his pale paws, and he muttered, *'Jes another slice – don' be shy wiff that jam ...'*

Willow felt her heart twist as she looked down at him. He hadn't really been himself lately either. His fur had faded, going from a bright lime green to a pale, washed-out khaki colour. There were even some patches of missing fur, which she'd been told were likely due to him worrying about her – and that made Willow feel terrible. So she left him to his dreams and his rest.

There was another reason, though, that Willow didn't want to wake Oswin. There was something she wanted to try, and she didn't want an audience. Or a lecture. Oswin was very fond of those.

Inside the hairy carpetbag was a broomstick that had been folded down to a quarter of its size with the help of some Elvish Reduction Rings. They resembled

brass curtain rings and had been fitted on each end of the broom. Through a complicated bit of elvish magic, the rings made the broom act a bit like an accordion, compacting down. She'd got them as a gift from her elvish friend, Twist, who tamed the north wind. Twist had visited her by tornado for tea a few weeks earlier and given her the rings so that Willow could always have her broom, Whisper, with her, ready for when she got her magic back.

Willow had been touched by Twist's faith just as much as she had been by the gift, which was incredibly useful at times like this: when she wanted to try flying in secret.

2

Return to the Tower

Willow held on to the elvish rings on each end of her broomstick and pulled until Whisper began to stretch before her eyes.

For a moment, she held her breath, her heart filled with hope . . . But the usual blue glow whenever her hands touched Whisper was gone. Even the tail end, full of pale, beautiful cloud-dragon feathers, was now a strange, dull grey; like a sad feather duster.

Even though it wasn't the first time she'd seen it like this, it brought a catch to Willow's throat.

She put the broom between her legs

and begged softly, 'Please, Whisper. Come back to life. Come back to . . . me.'

But nothing happened. Just as nothing had happened the day before or the day before that.

Willow tried a few more times, adding in a running leap and a jump or two, which just made her crash to her knees. She held out her arms to brace herself and went skidding into the dirt. Tears threatened, but she took a deep breath, raised her chin and dusted some of the mud off. She looked at Whisper as she would a dear but ill friend. 'We'll try again tomorrow.'

Then she had a silent word with her tear ducts, encouraging them to think of other things, like funny little elths who were overprotective of their currant buns.

Willow sighed. Brooms chose their owners by responding to the magic within them. She knew that at some point she should just give up, admit defeat and accept that her magic was really, truly gone, and that was why Whisper didn't work: it simply *couldn't*. But she kept hoping that a tiny seed of magic had been left behind, one that she just needed to coax into life . . .

The idea that Silas might soon break free and

attempt to finish what he'd started, and she wouldn't be able to stop him, just devastated her. It was why she had been doing everything she could think of to get her magic back.

Apart from trying to *will* it to return, she'd attempted all manner of other things as well.

A month before, Willow had visited the town of Library to search for information about magic loss with the help of a Secret Keeper and librarian named Copernica Darling. None of the books they'd found had said anything about how to actually get magic *back*, though, just that people who suffered magic loss often felt cold and tired – something Willow knew from experience already. It was the main reason she had left her draughty attic to share a room, once more, with her sister Camille. She'd spent a great deal of time there, wrapped in blankets and drinking hot tea.

While Willow had loved being back in the bookish town, it had been a disappointment. She'd been so sure the answer would be there among all those old tomes and scrolls. Copernica had promised that she'd keep looking, but she hadn't seemed very hopeful.

Willow had gone to bed that night feeling despondent, wishing that Granny Flossy were still alive. She couldn't help thinking that Granny might have had an idea – some potion experiment or plant remedy that could help . . . which was when she'd jumped out of bed, breathless with excitement, realising that perhaps her grandmother still *could*.

Willow had torn into the attic, where Granny Flossy used to sleep, and begun frantically searching for her notebook, where she had recorded all her potion experiments. In hindsight, Willow might have considered *not* taking the stairs at a gallop as it was well past midnight. Seconds later, her mother's sleepy face had appeared, demanding to know what on Great Starfell she was doing. When Willow had explained, her mother's face had fallen, and she'd told Willow something very unfortunate indeed – that she'd given the notebook to Granny Flossy's old potions partner.

'Um, this was before I knew that Amora Spell was a—'

'—conniving, thieving, backstabbing liar who caused the accident that ended Granny Flossy's career and took credit for her life's work?!' Willow had roared, utterly incensed.

'If yew wos a **kobold** like me, yeh'd 'ave exploded right then,' Oswin had pointed out.

Her mother had winced. 'Y-y-yes,' she'd admitted, mortified.

Perhaps it was seeing her mother look so abashed, but Willow's anger had deflated like an old balloon. 'I suppose you didn't know . . . but now what? We can't let that awful fraud keep it. We owe Granny that much.'

'You're right,' her mother said, which had been something of a surprise.

The next day, they'd gone to confront Amora at her last-known address. Willow had vowed to prise the notebook out of the old woman's pilfering hands if she had to – but they were too late. The trickster had moved on, and no one had seen or heard from her in months. Willow had been forced back to square one.

The following week, she had heard about a visiting wizard named Igh Falutin, who was said to be one of the few magic folk in Starfell who could still perform spells. Willow invited him over for tea, and he accepted rather quickly, perhaps not realising who her family were. It turned out that the only 'spell' he knew how to cast was fooling people into believing he

had any magic at all – just before he took their money and made a run for it. He didn't get far, though, as Willow's sisters soon caught up with him . . .

One of their neighbours reported that he had been blasted to smithereens, and another said that you could see his legs sticking out of a nearby farmhouse, but Willow was sure that those were just rumours.

Mostly sure.

She hadn't had time to check the nearby farmhouse for Igh Falutin's dangling legs because soon after she was nearly swindled by him the effects of her magic loss really started to catch up with her. Willow grew ill, feeling constantly cold and tired no matter how many jumpers she wore or how much sleep she got.

It was then that her mother and Moreg had decided it might be best to take her to a professional healer. Unfortunately, that professional healer turned out to be the hedge witch Blu-Scarly Pimpernell, whose enchanted tower deep in the heart of the Howling Woods hadn't been high up on Willow's list of Top Ten Places to Visit Ever Again . . .

. . . Considering the witch had once locked her up right at the very top and refused to let her out.

3

Odd Fruit

Despite Oswin's screeches – '**Oh no,** oh, me **greedy aunt! Anywhere** but that **infermerol place!**' – Willow's mother had forced the issue and taken Willow and Oswin to Pimpernell's tower.

But, whatever they might have thought before, so far – over the past two weeks – they had been looked after really well. Though eccentric and prone to taking things a bit too far, Pimpernell was good at what she did. She had given Willow a new tonic that not only contained wispdust but also helped to lessen some of the effects of magic loss, so at least she didn't feel completely exhausted and cold all the time. She still needed a lot more rest than usual, but she almost felt normal.

Staying at the tower was also a double protective measure against Silas. To Willow's surprise, she'd learnt that

the gold glitter covering the building was in fact a coating of wispdust, used by Pimpernell to protect her patients.

Willow was even having some fun, thanks mainly to Pimpernell's new assistant, Willow's friend Essential Jones. The Enchancil had appointed her so that the hedge witch didn't go about locking up any more people against their will, even if she insisted it was for their own good.

In the mornings, like today, Willow could go out for strolls in the woods to collect ingredients for remedies. And, of course, it gave her the opportunity to try flying Whisper.

For now, though, Willow shrank her broom back down to its compact size, slipped it into her bag, and sat under the fife tree. Then she popped another bark berry into her mouth – only to spit it out again because it was rotten. She frowned. It had *appeared* fresh. She tried another one, and it had turned too. That was strange. She'd never had that happen before – where a piece of fruit *looked* normal but tasted off.

Just then, from the sky above, a single perfect snowflake fluttered down. Willow blinked in surprise, then instinctively held out her hand to catch it. It landed gently in her palm and melted. She looked up at the sky, waiting for more, but nothing came.

23

Odd, she thought, before making her way back through the woods to Pimpernell's tower.

The tower sparkled in the sun. To be fair, it probably sparkled in the dark too, because it was covered in moons and stars and the wispdust glitter. Willow had always thought that it might have been subtler to have had a flashing neon sign that said: A WITCH LIVES HERE.

Just as Willow approached, the tower's door was flung open, and Essential Jones hurried out. She was a tall girl with brown skin and long curly hair. She used to be rather short, like Willow, but she'd grown several inches over the past year, though she still had the same thick glasses that always slipped down her nose.

'Willow! Finally! I've been looking for you. I've got rounds to do – I thought you wanted to come with me?'

Willow's eyes brightened. This, to be fair, wasn't most people's reaction to the idea of doing chores, but Willow wasn't like most people. She really enjoyed going on Essential's rounds, visiting Pimpernell's patients – witches and wizards with minor magical maladies who didn't need long-term care in the tower – to bring them tonics, potions and salves that the hedge witch had prepared.

The day before they'd helped someone who had been growing an onion out of their big toe.

An actual onion.

It was utterly, unbelievably gross. But also kind of brilliant. To Willow's surprise, she had enjoyed it. Well, not the toe onion exactly, but the fact she could help. It made her feel a bit like her old self, as in the past she'd spent most of her days using her magic to help reunite people with their lost belongings, and this felt a little like that. In fact, it was one of the first things Pimpernell had prescribed for Willow, sensing, perhaps more than her family had, that she'd been missing helping others almost as much as she missed her magic.

'I do want to come! I was just out collecting these bark berries for Pimpernell – she mentioned that she might need some soon to bulk up her supply of salves for magical misfires. She said it was one of the ingredients . . .' Willow patted her basket, then frowned. 'But I did notice something strange. Some of them taste rotten, but they look fresh. I'm not sure how we'll work out which ones are okay to use?'

Essential frowned and peered into the basket. 'Hmm, that is a bit weird. We'll mention it to Pimpernell when we're back – I'm sure she'll know.

We'd best be heading off, though. Let's go and pack the Ambulbroom!'

Unfortunately, this was the precise moment that Oswin chose to wake up. There was a harrumph, followed by the sound of the hairy carpetbag being unzipped, and he appeared, glaring at Willow.

'**Oi, wot is the meanerings of this?**' he hissed. '**I said I WOS goings fer a monster-nap. Not that I would likes ter be** *monsternapped*! '**Tis a big difference. Not even askings me if I wants ter come. No respect** – and me being the last kobold . . .'

Technically, this wasn't true. Oswin was the *second-to-last* kobold, but he didn't like to mention his cousin. He felt Osmeralda 'damaged' the 'good reputation' of kobolds by engaging in scandalous activities such as having a bath more than once a year.

Willow, who was used to his grumblings, shot him a look. 'So, should I leave you behind at the tower?'

There was another harrumph, louder than the first, at the idea of being abandoned, and Oswin crept back inside the bag, muttering darkly about '**completelys missing the points**'.

She took that as a no.

4

The Ambulbroom

After Willow had left her basket of bark berries in the kitchen, Essential led the way to a shed round the back of the tower.

The Ambulbroom was an incredibly long broomstick made out of a black, shiny wood that sparkled with moons and stars and, of course, gold glitter, just like the tower. It had four tall seats with green padded leather backs like dining-room chairs. If you pulled a lever, they folded down into stretcher beds – useful for when Pimpernell had to go and collect ailing witches and wizards.

Willow had fallen a little bit in love with the strange broom and longed to take it for a spin herself. She felt that familiar pang of loss, knowing that she *couldn't*, not without her magic.

Oswin grumbled from the hairy green carpetbag on Willow's arm. **'Oh, me greedy aunt, the on'y fing goods abouts yer not 'aving yer magic any more wos that I fought I din't has ter get on no more blooming flyin' sticks nohow, no way. . . Instead, we 'ave this JUMBO version.'**

'I know,' said Willow happily.

Oswin, however, had turned a sickly shade of green, and his eyes peeked above the carpetbag at her in guilt. He whispered, **'Sorry. I means . . . oh, me 'orrid aunt.'** He put his paws over his eyes.

It was a bit odd to see Oswin feeling bad about his outbursts. Willow knew that he didn't mean anything by them.

'It's fine, Os. I'm sure I'll get to ride Whisper again someday.'

Well, she hoped so. Willow swallowed, squashing down the fear that she might *never* get her magic back. She would. She had to.

Oswin still had his face buried in his paws, and was busy calling himself all manner of names. **'Blimmerings galumphing cumberworld . . .'**

Willow patted his head. 'I know how much you hate flying. You really can stay home if you want.'

'**No,**' he said protectively, finally removing his paws from his eyes. '**Yeh never knows oo yew is gonna run into. Yew might need some monster muscle.**'

As the 'monster muscle' appeared to resemble a large and rather frightened-looking tabby cat, Willow and Essential had to have a word with their faces to ensure that they didn't betray any doubts over this.

'Too right,' said Essential, only her voice came out in a very high squeak.

Oswin screwed up an eye to peer at her, just in case she was mocking him (he was highly sensitive and very attuned to any sort of insult), but after a while he grunted, satisfied.

There was a beeping sound and suddenly one of the levers on the side of the Ambulbroom came loose, and the four chairs suddenly fanned out all around it.

'Not again,' sighed Essential, putting them back in place.

The Ambulbroom flew for Essential because Pimpernell had sanctioned it, but it was a bit glitchy as it was a kind of borrowed magic; brooms much

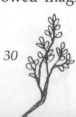

preferred to be ridden by their rightful owners.

Willow climbed on to a seat at the back with Oswin in the hairy carpetbag on her lap. The broom remained lifeless until Essential sat at the front, then it started to glow faintly blue. Essential took a pair of flying goggles out of her cloak and swapped her glasses for them. Then she pushed down with her feet, and the broom rose so fast it knocked Willow back into her seat, like she was on a roller coaster. Essential took out a scroll and scanned the list written there.

'Just a few stops today. Ooh, actually, this one might be good first,' she said, tapping the first line so that it magically moved down and the second line jumped to the top.

Before Willow could ask any questions, Essential said, 'Hold tight!' Then she lightly rapped the compass fixed on to the top of the broom handle with the scroll. The compass began to spin as it located the precise distance to the new first address. It stopped spinning when it found it, and Essential put the broom into gear. There were two settings: LIKE A BULLET and *Sunday stroll*.

She pushed the lever into the slot labelled LIKE A BULLET and they shot off instantly.

31

Unfortunately, travelling so fast wasn't exactly comfortable. The speeding broom created a kind of tunnel through the air, like they were the last bit of toothpaste being squeezed out of the tube.

Finally, the Ambulbroom reached its destination, and as they slowed down their surroundings came into focus.

'Oh, **me** 'orrid **aunt Osbertrude!**' cried Oswin. 'I swears **me** eyeballs jes went **frough me bum.**'

And, if that weren't bad enough, suddenly they

32

were being whipped across the sky by gusting winds
and torrential rain.

'Ah!' yelped Essential. 'We've been knocked a
bit off course by this weather, but we're almost
there!' she shouted, changing the broom's gear
to *Sunday stroll* and steering them towards the
thrashing river below and a familiar boat.

'Is that the *Sudsfarer*?' asked Willow, but the wind
and rain snatched her words away as they hurtled
towards a large copper boat that looked like a bathtub,

33

coming into land far too fast.

The next thing Willow knew, they were all flying off the Ambulbroom and sliding along the slippery deck. Willow landed on her bottom and managed not to fall over the side by bracing herself against the boat's railings with her legs.

But Oswin wasn't so lucky. He went flying overboard, yelling, **'A curse upon yew!'**

Reacting fast, Essential held out both hands and used her magic to slow down Oswin's plunge into the water. Spying a rather large copper fishing net, Willow raced to fetch it and swung it over the side of the boat as quickly as she could, scooping the sopping-wet kobold out of the water.

'Oh, m-me greedy **aunt**,' Oswin said weakly, through chattering teeth, his soaked fur making him look half his usual size.

'Thanks, Essential!' Willow cried over the wind, grateful that the kobold was safe. 'You're getting so good with your magic.'

Essential had been gaining better control over her ability to freeze things in time, and now she could make the freezes last a bit longer and even cause things to move in slow motion as well as stop them altogether. Willow was proud of her friend, so she pushed down the twinge of pain she felt at the absence of her own magic.

By now, they were all so drenched that there were puddles inside their shoes, and Willow's hair resembled wet curtains on either side of her face. They fished Oswin out of the net and held on to each other for support as the wind tried its best to toss them overboard too.

A *rap-tap-tap* on the window behind them made them jump.

They turned to find Holloway, the wizard captain of the *Sudsfarer*, looking out at them from the cabin, a worried expression in his one sea-green eye.

5

Holloway's Confession

Holloway beckoned them hastily inside. They opened the wooden door that led below deck, which was almost torn off its hinges in the gale. Willow hung on for dear life to try and shut it again behind them. They clattered down the copper steps and crowded inside, where the happy-looking whale on the welcome mat lost its smile as it was doused in the cascade of water sheeting from their clothes.

The boat rocked precariously, and Oswin moaned, **'Oh, me 'orrid aunt, this is jes not me day. I fink I'm gonna lose me lunch, except I 'aven't even 'ad any yet.'**

Holloway whipped off one of his dragon-scale gloves and touched the boat. 'Steady there, *Sudsfarer*, steady now.'

And it felt for a moment like the boat had found its feet – which it may well have done, considering Willow knew it had four of them paddling under the water.

Holloway hastily put his glove back on, then smiled at his visitors. 'Willow, Essential and Oswin! 'Tis great to see ya,' he said.

Willow had first met the old captain during her first stay at Pimpernell's tower, and Essential had met him not long afterwards, when he'd helped them to rescue their friend Nolin Sometimes from the ghostly ruler of Netherfell.

Holloway opened his arms as if to hug them, then paused, a reluctant expression passing over his face. 'Er, one sec,' he said, then rushed off to fetch several fluffy pink-and-green towels. He passed them round, and Willow pressed one with a starfish pattern to her sopping face gratefully.

'What brings ya here? Not that I mind, but didn't think I'd get any company with this storm,' said Holloway, beginning to towel down Oswin – to his absolute horror.

'**Oi! Wot choo fink yer doin'?**' he yelped, shooting Holloway a shocked look. Then he quickly

shook his fur out like a dog, and water droplets that smelt a bit like mouldy socks and cooked cabbage went flying everywhere, making them all groan.

'Watch it!' cried Essential, rubbing her steamed-up glasses on her sodden dress. She hung up her cloak on the peg behind her and shivered, then turned to Holloway. 'We came to bring you your medicine,' she explained.

'Medicine?' Willow asked, concerned, as she towelled her own hair. 'You all right, Holloway?'

'Fit as a fiddle, lass. Well, apart from the fact that, as you know, I turn everything to copper,' he said, holding up his gloved hands, 'and unfortunately the copper has been having a bit of an effect on me insides. But Pimpernell has come up with a great tonic that makes sure it doesn't, ya know . . .'

'. . . Poison you?' asked Willow, eyes wide.

'Pretty much.'

'Here it is,' said Essential, finding the small bottle in her cloak and handing it over.

'Ta, lass. Ya don't need to run off just yet, do ya? Time for a cuppa – warm them bones?'

Willow slipped off her cloak, and something

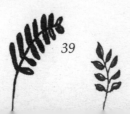

went clattering to the floor. It was the StoryPass, a device that had been made in the town of Library. It was originally meant for novel cataloguing, but often gave useful life advice too, like: *'If I Were You, I'd Run'*, *'One Might Have Suspected as Such'*, *'Turning Point'*, *'There be Dragons'* and *'Cup of Tea?'*

Right then it *was* suggesting tea. Willow grinned and picked up the StoryPass. She was soaking wet, and, especially given how easily she got cold and tired these days, she had to admit that a cup of tea with an

old friend in front of the log burner was incredibly inviting. 'Sounds good to me,' she said.

'Yes, let's wait out the storm before we head off to see our next patient,' suggested Essential.

'Great,' said Holloway, hanging their wet cloaks to dry in front of the fire and inviting them to sit in a pair of comfy armchairs. 'Sit, sit. I'll pop the kettle on.'

When he came back with a tea tray, he set it down and took a seat on a small green pouffe with a bit of a grunt. He rubbed a nervous hand over his face.

'I'm glad you're here, Willow, but I have to admit I didn't know what I was going to say to ya when I did see ya again.' His eye was full of pity.

Willow's heart sank. She bit her lip, guessing what he was likely to say and eager to head him off. 'Don't worry about me, Holloway. I'm a bit, um, tired, but otherwise I'm okay,' she lied.

But she wasn't. Not at all. No one really understood what it was like having your magic taken from you . . . the loss she felt and the pain. She might not have been able to blow things up or move impossibly heavy things with her mind like her sisters, but she had used her ability every day to help people. Her

magic was a part of her, like her nut-brown hair or the way her eyes turned up at the corners. Coping without it was like living with a chronic illness. You didn't just 'get better'. You learnt to manage it.

She hated it whenever someone told her how sorry they were to hear about the loss of her magic. People acted weirdly about it. Either they called her brave for managing to simply exist, or they hounded her with questions, making her even more exhausted than she already was. Willow often felt like she was some kind of peculiar creature they were examining beneath a microscope.

There was another reason, though, that she didn't like talking about it: guilt.

Willow and her friends had been tricked by Silas. When a priceless scroll had been stolen from the town of Library – a scroll that no one had been able to translate for millennia but was rumoured to contain the location of a lost kingdom where the powerful elf staff was hidden – they'd believed that Silas had cracked the code and was close to finding the long-lost device. The staff was known to have two sides, one dark and one light: it could grant magic powers, and it could take them away. They had believed that if they didn't get there first Silas would seize the staff and use it to rip every bit of magic out of Starfell.

But it was all a ruse. Silas had just wanted them to *think* that he'd been able to translate the scroll, so that Willow would summon the lost kingdom, using her magic, and lead him right to the elf staff. And Willow and her friends had fallen for it.

So she hated it when people were sorry for her. Willow felt to blame for all of it. Hadn't she caused her own magic loss? Didn't she deserve it, in a way, after putting so many lives at risk?

But now it wasn't just pity she could see on Holloway's face.

'Oh, lass,' said the wizard, his eye filling with tears. 'Yer magic going is all my fault!'

6

Storm Light

They all looked at Holloway in surprise.

'What?' cried Willow.

Holloway set down his mug of knotweed tea with a thud and put his head in his gloved hands.

'Holloway,' said Willow, '*how* could it possibly be your fault?'

He gasped. 'How can ya say that? If it weren't for me, none of this would have happened!' He shot them all a fierce look, his sea-green eye blazing as he pointed to his glass one. 'If I hadn't given Rubix me old clouded eye, Silas wouldn't have stolen it from her and been able to mask what he was planning from Moreg Vaine, the greatest seer in Starfell! If she'd known what he was up to, he wouldn't have been able to trick ya into finding the lost elvish kingdom or the

staff, or drained yer magic . . .'

'That's a lot of "wouldn't-haves",' said Willow kindly.

She knew that Holloway had once had a strange, magical clouded eye that he could pop easily out of its socket. It had made the world look grey and miserable, so he had traded it with Rubix Grimoire, the witch who had raised Essential since she was a baby. He hadn't known that the eye, whether worn or carried, could keep its owner hidden from witches and wizards who had the ability to see the future.

'You weren't to know any of that would happen,' Willow went on. 'Who's to say Silas wouldn't have found a clouded eye somewhere else anyway? Then the same thing would've happened. *I'm* the one who should've known better.'

'You *really* can't blame yourself, Holloway. You gave Rubix your clouded eye years ago,' Essential added.

He sighed, then shook his head. 'I can't believe I thought it was useless! How could I not have known that's what me own blimmin' eye did?'

There was a nod of deep understanding from the monster from under the bed.

45

'I knows jes wot yer means,' said Oswin. 'I 'ad this weirds 'ard fing on me bum fer ever, and it wos drivin' me bonkers wonderings wot it wos. Some kobolds used ter 'ave horns that opened up the door ter fairyland . . . and I fought mebbe this wos mine coming in or sumfink?'

'What?' breathed Willow.

He nodded again. 'Like o' course mine *woulds* be on me backside wiff my luck . . . but then the other day I 'ad a good scratch and it came offs, and it wos jes a lemon drop.'

They all stared at him.

'And yew know,' he said with a grin, 'me luck 'ad changed cos it wos still pretty tasties, considering.'

'Ew!' Willow and Essential grimaced.

Holloway stared at the kobold. 'I suppose that's . . . erm . . . similar?'

The tiniest laugh escaped from Essential, who clapped a hand over her mouth immediately. But this only made Willow press her lips together to stop herself from laughing too. Even Holloway did a few facial gymnastics of his own.

But it was too late. Soon they were all in hysterics.

Holloway's eye started leaking in mirth. He slapped

his knee. 'Oh, kobold, ya might not mean to but ya certainly have a talent for lightening the mood!'

Oswin looked a bit disgruntled. **'Yer welcome?'**

Which made them laugh even harder. It felt good to laugh.

Willow looked at the old sailor. 'But honestly, Holloway, the truth is that *no one* knew your clouded eye blocked a seer's visions, apart from Moreg herself.'

'Who, let's face it, isn't exactly normal,' added Essential.

This was true. Moreg Vaine was one of the most powerful and infamous witches in all of Starfell. Willow hadn't seen her for a while, as she was busy working with Celestine Bear and the rest of the Enchanted Council – or Enchancil – on preparations for Silas's possible return.

'Even Rubix didn't know,' Essential continued.

'The point is, you can't blame yourself,' said Willow.

'Nor can yew,' said Oswin.

Willow swallowed. She hadn't realised it was so obvious.

'If that's true fer Cap'n Hollobobs, then it's true fer yew too.'

Willow looked away. It was harder for her to forgive herself than to forgive others. Besides, as far as she was concerned, what Holloway did was different. He'd had no way of predicting what would happen because of his actions, whereas Willow had *known* that she was bringing back one of the most powerful tools in Starfell's history. Yes, she'd been tricked into doing it, but it was still hard not to feel a sense of shame that she hadn't even wondered, not once, if unearthing the elf staff from where it had lain, undisturbed, for a thousand years was really the right way to protect it from Silas. It was the first thing that came to mind when she woke up and the last thing she thought about before falling, fitfully, to sleep at night.

It was one of the reasons why she so desperately wanted her magic back. She had to get the staff away from Silas. To right what she had done wrong.

But Willow didn't say any of that. She knew her friends wouldn't want her to feel bad, so she changed the subject. She'd been getting rather good at that.

They chattered and enjoyed their tea, and Holloway surprised them with some rain biscuits, which cheered them all up considerably. They were soft and buttery and tasted of rainstorms and honeysuckle.

Willow explained to Essential how they were made using rainwater that bounced off the Knotweed River, giving them their distinctive flavour.

'Ya know,' said Holloway, 'a funny thing happened, actually, when I tried to make them earlier. I collected the rainwater as usual and made me first batch, but they tasted *awful* – sour and metallic. Not sure why. I had to use some old rainwater I froze a few weeks ago for these.'

'That's strange,' said Willow. She thought for a moment of the unpleasant surprise *she'd* had that morning, with the rotten-tasting bark berries.

Holloway nodded, then shrugged. 'Though it has been one heck of a storm, so maybe something has been stirred up from the riverbed.'

A little while later Essential fetched their cloaks, handing Willow hers, then went to get the Ambulbroom ready. Willow drained her cup and gave Holloway a farewell kiss on the top of his head.

'Hang on, got something for ya,' said Holloway as he and Willow stepped out on to the deck and she slipped on her dried cloak. He went back to fetch something from the cabin. It was a tiny, perfect copper lighthouse.

49

'It's called a storm light. It glows ten times brighter than you'd think it could for its size.' He tapped it and the whole bridge filled with amber light. 'Reminds me of you. How strong ya are despite yer size. Ye'll get through this, lass, I know ya will. And I know ya don't want to accept it, but the kobold is right – this isn't all on you. We all had a part to play – that's what Silas was counting on. Right now, we just have to make sure that we play another part: making sure he doesn't get away with it again.'

Willow bit her lip to stop herself from crying. 'Thank you, Holloway,' she said, struggling to find the words past the lump in her throat. She'd needed to hear that more than she could say. 'The storm light is beautiful. I'll treasure it.'

They had time to wave goodbye just once more before they shot off again on the Ambulbroom, with the gear set to LIKE A BULLET .

'Oh, me greedy aunt Osbertrude! I knows jes wot a sausage feels like now, and it ain't pretty,' moaned Oswin.

7

Unexpected Tidings

As they entered a small village with rolling green hills and sheep grazing in the distance, Essential set the broom to (*Sunday stroll*) so they could recover from their somewhat uncomfortable journey.

But, as they slowed down, Willow noticed that scattered here and there were large black patches scarring the hillsides.

'That's odd. I wonder what those are?' she asked, pointing.

Essential turned to look, but, before she could reply, they heard a loud cawing overhead, and Willow saw a raven circling above. Its wings glittered like it was dusted with gold.

'Oh!' said Essential. 'It's the raven Pimpernell uses for the post – I'd recognise that glitter anywhere. She

must have sent it after us with a note.'

They flew to meet the bird, who perched on the end of the long broomstick handle, allowing Essential to take the letter from its claws.

'Thanks, Frank,' said Essential, and the raven flew away.

Then she frowned at the letter she'd opened. 'It's from Rubix – Pimpernell will have sent it on. It must be important.'

Rubix Grimoire, Essential's guardian, was also the editor of the *Grimoire Gazette* and a senior member of the Enchancil. Willow knew it was possible she would have news of Silas.

'What does it say?' asked Willow anxiously.

'Read it for yourself – she's addressed it to you too.'

Dearest Essential and Willow,

I hope that things with Pimpernell are going smoothly. Here are the headlines from me.

The Howling sisters – the aunts of Willow's elvish friend, Twist – came to visit last week. We got into a dispute when I suggested the elves

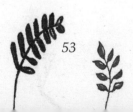

53

need to arrange a truce with the trolls so that we can all work together to fight Silas. They made it rain inside my house at the idea. Tensions between the two communities are at an all-time high since part of Troll Country was taken up by the ancient elvish kingdom that reappeared from underground. Technically, this means it was always there, but the trolls aren't seeing it that way at all. (They're attempting to take land from Dwarf Territory to make up for the loss – though, of course, they try that every year. The dwarfs aren't having it.)

Willow winced at this, considering she was the one who'd brought the kingdom of Llandunia back. It made the hard knot of guilt inside her grow to know the trolls, elves and dwarfs were fighting because of it. She kept reading.

Ultimately, despite their frustration, the elves have now assured the Enchancil they will work as a team with the trolls. This is in part due to the fact that Celestine Bear has agreed that elves can have a seat on the Enchancil again for the first time in fifty years.

This hasn't been received well by all – the elves, as you know, are not known for their tact when they think an idea is stupid. Not to mention that some are afraid that they will use their weather abilities to fry people with lightning again. The Howling sisters have sworn to rein in their tempers. This is good advice for us all. Now the threat that Silas poses to us has been exposed, it is more important than ever for magical folk to be united. We are hopeful that troll chief Megrat and dwarf king Zazie may come to a peace agreement.

The Enchancil is also working with the broom-makers, the Mementons, to ensure that all magical people have some form of quick transportation in case a militant band of the Brothers of Wol start rounding up more witches and wizards.

As you may have heard, after Silas was captured, some of the Brothers were released from the Gerful chalk he had been using to control them. A few, on realising what had happened, were grateful to the magical community for setting them free and have begun working with the Enchancil –

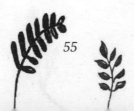

but, alas, most of them refused to believe that magical folk could ever be trusted and remain loyal to their missing leader. We are still trying to reason with them, but, as they have once again taken refuge in the fortress of Wolkana, which is impenetrable to all magic, it is difficult to establish a line of communication. Each time we try, they attack our envoys with flaming arrows.

No news of Silas as yet. Hopefully, the rock dragons are proving too strong for him.

'I'm glad some of the Brothers of Wol have started to work with the Enchancil,' observed Essential, pushing up her glasses. 'I just wish the rest would see sense.'

'When it comes ter **magic**, those cumberworlds 'aven't seen sense fer eleventy-billy-bob years. Not sures why they'd try bovvering wiff it now,' said Oswin.

He had a point. The Brothers of Wol had been a force against magic for over a thousand years. They spread word that it was evil and unnatural – an affliction that needed to be stamped out.

Silas, whose father used to be High Master of the Brothers of Wol, had been raised with these beliefs

too – even though he himself was born with a fizz of magic. When he was a baby, his witch mother, Molsa, had died, and Molsa's sister, Moreg Vaine, had placed him in the care of his father, believing it could lead to the Brothers of Wol opening their minds to magic. Instead, Silas had been filled with shame, and over the years he had become twisted and vengeful.

When Silas uncovered the secret that Wol, the 'god' they worshipped, had been a wizard too, he was inspired to complete what the former magician had started. He hoodwinked the Brothers, pretending he wanted to stamp out magic, when instead he plotted to steal it all for himself – aiming to become as powerful as Wol, as powerful as a *god*, so they would worship him. Clearly, many of the Brothers were still under that illusion.

'It's good news that even *some* of them have seen the truth,' Willow said, and they kept reading Rubix's letter.

The only other news is a bit closer to home. For some reason, the entire area around the Midnight Market has gone under permanent darkness. My own house, just a mile away, is perfectly fine – the sun is still rising and setting as it always has.

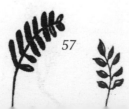

57

It must be some sort of rogue magic? Perhaps one of the stallholders did something to encourage the market's nefarious reputation.

Speaking of strange, nefarious things, I ran into Amora Spell the other night. I know she used to be your granny's potions partner, Willow. She's returned to her old potions stall, though it has undergone some transformations! I must admit I was never much of a fan of hers, but as she was a family friend I thought you might be interested to know that she's back. I must say I always thought she was a bit of a fraud, but perhaps I was wrong, as I've never seen her stall so busy or popular, and full of such new and exciting potions. Thought you might want to know, Willow, as I am aware you were looking for a cure for your stolen magic. Maybe she can help? Anyway, must get on with the latest edition of the *Grimoire Gazette* – the gist of which I've shared with you already, so at least you're the first to hear.

Stay safe and stay out of trouble.

With love,

Rubix Grimoire

When Willow got to the end of the letter, she cried out in excitement. 'Amora Spell – Rubix has found her!'

Clearly, Willow's mother hadn't told Rubix *everything*, or she would have known that her granny's old partner was a fraud and a cheat, and that Rubix was spot on about there being something very iffy about her.

Oswin snatched the letter and read the last paragraph himself, turning blood orange in the process. **'Not 'ard ter guess why she's suddenlies so popular.'**

'I know!' said Willow, who – to both Essential and Oswin's surprise – looked delighted by this turn of events.

Smoke began to furl off the top of Oswin's head. **'Stall fulls o' new potions – yew know 'ow she suddenlies got that, right? She's using the Flossy Mistress's old potion experiments!'**

Willow nodded.

'**An' yew is 'appy abouts this?**' asked Oswin, raising his eyebrows.

Willow shook her head. 'Not happy about her being a fraud, a liar and a cheat, *no*, but I am happy, yes, because now we know where to find her.'

Oswin sighed. '**Oh, me greedy aunt, I should 'ave knowns yew wos gonna say that.**'

Willow looked at Essential. 'I know it specifically says to stay safe and stay out of trouble . . .'

Essential cocked her head. 'But you want to do the opposite?'

'Pretty much, yes.'

They grinned at each other.

'Fair enough,' said Essential, lips twitching. She glanced at her list of patients. 'Norman Verbena still has bubbles coming out of his mouth. I've told him time and again that the solution is to stop taking anti-balding potion, but he never listens. I think he can suffer the consequences a little longer, don't you?'

Willow's grin widened.

Essential put the list in her pocket. 'Let's prise that notebook from the hands of that—'

'Harpy-hag?' suggested Oswin.

'Harpy-hag,' Essential confirmed.

Willow smiled. 'Sounds like a plan.'

8

The Hurting Sky

As Willow, Essential and Oswin approached the Midnight Market, Willow geared herself up to confront Amora Spell.

Essential had set the Ambulbroom to *Sunday stroll* so that they could see the changes that Rubix had described – how the market area had suddenly been plunged into permanent darkness.

'Oh no! Oh *nooooo*, oh, me greedy aunt!' cried Oswin, peeking out of the carpetbag. 'This ain't night-time!'

'What do you mean?' asked Willow.

Essential parked the broom in mid-air so they could get a better look at the line between night and day. It was a little like the way a single cloud could cast a shadow below, while the rest of the world was in sunlight.

'**This** ain't nights. 'Tis **sumfink** else,' Oswin whimpered.

Oh dear, thought Willow, swallowing. She shared an apprehensive glance with Essential. The ability to detect dangerous magic was part of Oswin's kobold heritage.

'Is it some strange magic? Is it harmful?'

'**I don' fink** so . . . 'tis more like **it's** hurt.'

'What's hurt?' Willow frowned.

'**The skies,**' said Oswin.

Willow and Essential stared. Willow hadn't known the sky could *be* hurt.

Oswin peered up at them with sad eyes. '**'Tis growing,** I fink, that hurt . . .'

'Growing?' breathed Willow.

Oswin pointed, and she saw the corner of the shadowy darkness stretch, ever so slightly, then swell as it took one more inch of the day around the Midnight Market.

'Great Starfell! What's making this happen?'

'**I don' know,**' he whispered.

'Rubix said she thought it was one of the stallholders, didn't she?' said Essential. 'That they'd used magic to do this on purpose?'

Willow looked at her uncertainly. 'But that's when

they just thought it was night. And Rubix didn't say anything about the darkness growing . . . If Oswin's right and it's some sort of sickness, we need to tell someone . . . maybe Moreg.'

'You definitely think it's safe for us to go?' Essential asked the kobold, and he nodded.

They flew down towards the tents and painted caravans, above the string lights that floated in the air, giving the market a festive albeit rather creepy air, like a haunted funfair. Essential brought the Ambulbroom down next to a large tree and leant it against the trunk.

As she did, Willow heard a low moaning sound. She saw what looked like odd black spots all over the bark of the tree – just like the ones she'd noticed in the Howling Woods near the tower earlier. *Strange*, she thought. She touched the spots with a frown. The tree shifted away from her fingers.

'Sorry,' she whispered.

The tree seemed to shrug, and for a moment she saw what looked like sad knots for eyes in its trunk.

'Are you all right?' she asked.

In answer, the tree closed its knot eyes, then opened them.

Willow had learnt not so long ago that some trees could walk and talk and move, but perhaps they couldn't when they were ill. It was a terrible thought.

'Are you hurt?'

The eyes blinked twice. Did that mean yes?

'I **fink** all o' this dark place is **hurt** really,' said Oswin. 'The **sky**, the trees ... sumfink is 'arming it.'

Willow blinked. Was he right?

'This might sound crazy,' said Essential slowly, 'but don't you think a few things have been a bit . . . off lately? Not just the dark sky and this tree, but other stuff too. Those weird berries you tasted this morning,

Willow, and Holloway's Knotweed River water too?'

'Yes, and those odd black scars on the hills we flew past earlier,' Willow recalled. 'And I saw another tree that looked speckled and sick like this one, near Pimpernell's tower!'

'But what can it mean?' Essential was puzzled. 'They're all in different places. Is it just a coincidence?'

Willow didn't know. 'I can't see how they link either. Just lots of things in nature being a bit . . . out of sorts. Maybe it's something to do with the weather?'

Essential nodded. 'Could be. It's been a cold winter.'

Willow touched the sick tree. 'Maybe we can help somehow?'

The tree looked at her, then blinked twice.

'I know a botanist – he might be able to help. I'll ask him to come, all right?'

The tree just stared at her. Maybe it had run out of energy to answer.

Willow frowned when a snowflake drifted in front of her, but, before she could really stop and wonder how this had happened *again*, she was distracted by Essential.

She shook Willow's arm and said, 'Look! I think I

67

can see Amora's tent from here. Come on – let's go. We can send Nolin Sometimes a message when we get home, ask him to investigate.'

Willow turned to where Essential was pointing and gasped.

The last time they'd seen Amora's stall it was a ramshackle thing that seemed to be on the verge of collapse, but this was something else. It was enormous and striped like a circus tent, with a long queue of people waiting outside. A huge airborne sparkler was busy writing enormous words in the air above it.

Amora Spell: Starfell's BEST Potion Master

This was followed by several daily specials in smaller sky sparkles:

Glamour – change yourself or whoever you wish!*

Strength – feel what it's like to really be as strong as an ox!**

Invisibility – have the power to go wherever you want without detection!***

And many more – all available as Amazing Potion Throws – the great Amora's own invention! Throw them at your enemies! No need for trickery.

*Lasts for fifteen minutes – no refunds!
**Side effects vary – including horns and occasional ox-head appearance.
***Can sometimes take a year to wear off, with various body parts becoming visible at different stages (best suited to the witch or wizard with a Stealth or Racer broom).

Anger flooded Willow's senses, drowning out everything else, including her worry over the poor tree and the surrounding countryside. Amora was profiting from her granny's inventions, claiming them all as her own.

Inside her pocket, the StoryPass suggested *One Might Have Suspected as Such*.

'The ol' **harpy-hag** ain't jes **gonna** gives this notebook **away wiffout a kerfuffle**,' Oswin pointed out, then flexed his slightly rusty-looking claws for emphasis.

Willow sighed. The kobold had a point. She turned to them both. 'We're going to have to cause a distraction, I think, so I can slip inside and try to find it.'

The light of an idea glimmered in her eyes as she looked down at Oswin speculatively.

He frowned. '**Wot yew lewking at me like that fer?**' he demanded, turning faintly pumpkin. '**Oi! I ain't fallin' fer *that*. Not agin.**'

Willow grinned. 'I don't know what you're talking about, Oswin. By the way, you're such a pretty . . . *cat*.'

Smoke curled off the top of his head. '**I is not a CA – Oi!**' He narrowed his eyes. '**I jes said I is NOT fallin' fer it. We 'as spoken abouts the C word.**'

As a kobold, one of Oswin's abilities was that he could explode . . . when he got upset enough. It didn't hurt him. In fact, it sometimes made him

feel a bit better afterwards.

Cottoning on to Willow's plan, Essential said, 'Aw, sorry, Oswin. Is kitty getting upset?'

'KITTY? HOW DARES YEW!' hollered Oswin, jumping out of the hairy carpetbag, his fur now pumpkin orange.

Willow looked at Essential with new respect. Even she had never dared go *that* far.

He turned to glare at the pair of them. 'If yew wants me ter blimmerings explode ON PORPOISE, all yew 'as ter do is asks.'

'You can do that?' said Willow in surprise.

'Course.'

'Oh sorry, Oswin,' she said sheepishly. 'I didn't know.'

He glared at Essential. 'Yew an' me is not finished,' he told her.

Willow noticed that the long, snaking queue in front of them had started to dissipate as people went in and out of the tent. 'She's sorry, as am I. Please, please go and explode.'

He looked at them both through narrowed eyes, then harrumphed. 'Fine, but I is on'y doing it cos I wants ter, not cos I 'as ter.'

Then he skittered towards the tent door and waited. He closed his eyes like he was meditating, concentrating hard.

Nothing happened. He opened one eye. The people in the queue were all looking at him.

'Aw, look! Is the little pussycat going for a love potion?' one of them sniggered.

'Don't think Amora offers them any more, but he probably needs one, poor fella. Mangy-looking mog,' said another.

'Oh, fer FEET'S SAKE, FER THE LAST BLIMMERINGS TIME, I IS NOT A CAT!' Oswin hollered – then exploded, turning into a great orange fireball, rolling across the walkway, causing people to scream and flee in panic.

Reappearing in his catlike form, Oswin looked at Willow and Essential and blew on his claws before sheathing them. **'Cats can'ts do that, now can they?'**

Despite herself, Willow grinned. Though her smile died quickly as she realised Oswin had exploded a little too close to the tent, and the side wall had caught alight.

'Whoopsies,' he breathed.

From inside the tent, they could hear screaming, and a stream of people rushed out. Then they heard a gush of water dousing the flames from the inside.

'What's going on?' Amora cried, racing out of the tent with her bucket of water to check the damage.

Willow didn't stick around to be spotted. She took that moment, while Amora was distracted, to slip inside the tent, coughing a little from the lingering

smoke. Essential and Oswin followed at her heels, and together they began frantically searching the fully stocked tent for the notebook, pulling out drawers and looking under tables.

Essential grabbed Willow's hairy carpetbag and started putting potion bottles inside. 'Considering all of these are actually your granny's inventions, I don't feel the least bit bad pinching them.'

Willow nodded. 'Good thinking. Wish we had a bigger bag!'

'I'll stock up. You find the notebook.'

Willow nodded again, searching a chest of drawers at the back of the tent.

Suddenly a high, cold voice behind them said, 'And what do you think you're doing, dearies?'

9

Potions and Revelations

The hair on Willow's neck stood on end.

She turned slowly round, and Amora Spell was there, smiling. It was a cold smile that didn't reach her eyes. 'Jealous of me success, are you?' Amora's eyes glittered like insects in the dark. 'I see you've helped yourselves ter me things.' She shook her head. 'Can't be having that now, can we?'

'*Your* success? *Your* things?' Willow hissed. 'These are all Granny Flossy's inventions, which you're pretending are your own.'

To her surprise, Amora Spell grinned. 'Ah yes.' Then she took out a familiar notebook from her showy new coat, which was red and lined with gold silk. 'I was a bit surprised that Raine sent me Flossy's experiments, but then again yer mum never was that bright. Must run

in the family, eh, lass? I mean, I heard about yer little kerfuffle with Silas . . . Daft thing you did, bringing that kingdom back and unleashing the elf staff on the world. I mean, what kind of a fool wouldn't realise it was a trick? One of Flossy Mossy's grandbabies, that's who, I suppose – one who was allowed ter run amok with me old dingbat of a partner . . .'

It felt as if Willow had swallowed flames, and they tore through her till she was almost vibrating with rage. 'You can insult me, but don't you *dare* call Granny a dingbat.'

'I suppose she was actually quite something back in the day,' admitted Amora, 'before she went doolally. She might have prevented you from almost destroying the world . . . Well, I suppose you got yer punishment when yer magic was ripped out of you. Serves you right. Not that it was much magic ter begin with . . .'

'**Wot?**' yelled Oswin, turning blood orange. '**Yew cumberworld!**'

Willow's face was mottled with anger. 'At least I *had* magic, and did something with it! I didn't pretend to be someone I wasn't!' Then she snatched up several potion bottles off the nearby tables and launched one at the old woman – just as Amora took a small bottle filled with shimmering black liquid from her coat and lobbed it at them.

Essential held out her hands just in time, using her magical ability to slow it down in mid-air. She and Willow dodged out of the way, and the bottle cascaded gently and harmlessly to the floor in a puff of smoke.

Amora, however, had changed: she now had a giant ox's head instead of her own. 'You gave me strength?' she said, laughing. 'Daft thing.'

Willow and the others cringed.

Oswin whispered, **'Oh no.'**

And then Amora went to move – but couldn't. She frowned. On the floor was another broken potion throw called 'Wait'.

Amora sighed. 'Drat.'

Willow grinned, relieved.

'Not so daft after all,' said Essential with a grin.

Amora rolled her eyes, which looked particularly odd because they were now in an ox head.

'I must say I am surprised ter find you here,' said Amora, continuing their conversation as if they hadn't started launching potions at each other and she wasn't speaking from an ox's mouth. 'I would 'ave thought that you'd be in the mountains, trying ter find that beast, trying ter get yer magic back so you can make more messes the grown-ups have ter clean up.'

Guessing that she was speaking about Silas and the rock dragons, Willow sneered. 'Grown-ups like you? The only thing you've ever done is lie, cheat and steal.'

Not waiting for a response, Willow threw another potion called 'Forget', which exploded at the woman's feet.

'*Forget* everything you've ever learnt from Granny Flossy!'

Then Willow dived forward and snatched the notebook out of the woman's hands.

Amora was looking at her in confusion. 'What's going on?'

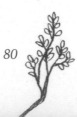

Which was when Essential threw another potion called 'Sleep', and Amora crumpled to the floor.

'Let's get out of here!' Willow hesitated for a second. 'I wish there was a potion that could make her grow a conscience or realise how truly evil she's been.'

'Yeh, **wells**, magic **only** goes so far,' said Oswin wisely, and he somehow managed to squish himself back inside the carpetbag alongside the potion bottles. '**Now let's skedaddle.**'

And they did.

10

Granny Flossy's Notebook

Through dinner, and while Willow had helped Pimpernell and Essential to dispense medicine, salves and ointments to the hedge witch's patients in the tower, it felt like Granny Flossy's notebook was whispering in her ear, calling her to come and read it.

She knew Essential wanted to look at it as well, but was too polite to ask. The notebook was a personal thing of Granny's, and Willow felt that the first time she read it she needed to do so alone. Partly because she was sure that she might just cry. Tears were never that far away whenever she handled something that used to belong to her granny.

After her duties were finished, Willow gave letters to the raven, Frank: one to her botanist friend, Nolin

Sometimes, hoping he could offer advice about the sick countryside, and the other to Moreg. If anyone might know what had happened to the Midnight Market, it was likely to be her – and, if she didn't, she needed to be informed that something very strange was going on.

Then, finally, Willow was able to wish Essential goodnight and turn in.

Essential smiled at her before they went to bed and said, 'I hope you find what you're looking for, Willow.'

Willow was touched. 'Thank you. Well, not just for that but for everything. Especially today.'

Essential pushed up her glasses, which were slipping off her nose. 'Taking down Amora was a definite highlight . . . especially when she thought she'd been given strength only to find herself stuck looking like a silly ox.'

Willow giggled. 'Yes. Though my favourite moment, apart from that and getting the notebook, of course, might have been when you called Oswin "kitty".'

They started to get the giggles. And, as is the case for most young girls giggling late at night, it wasn't long before someone was yelling that it was now, 'Time for bed!' This came from Pimpernell, accompanied

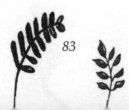

by the familiar *clink-clank-clink* sound of the hedge witch's copper foot against the floorboards, followed by a thud.

Willow mouthed one more 'goodnight' to Essential before she slipped away.

Her own room was small, with an iron bed on either side of a little wooden table beneath a window.

Willow's roommate, an old woman named Daisy Lea, suffered from arthritis and a curse that made her turn into a golden retriever every day when the sun went down. Oddly enough, she was only there for her arthritis . . . Right now, Daisy was fast asleep, curled up in a ball on the bed, yipping and running in the air occasionally while she snored.

Oswin, it must be said, had not been thrilled about sharing a room with a part-time dog, but Willow thought that Daisy made the ideal roommate – apart from when she barked or farted in her sleep. But then she supposed no one was perfect.

Willow climbed into bed, moving Oswin, who was also snoring, off her pillow, and then opened up the notebook at last.

Her heart was beating fast. She knew she shouldn't pin all her hopes of finding a cure for her magic on this book, but she couldn't help it.

She touched the cover, almost reverently. She had so many memories of seeing Granny Flossy with it while they had worked together in the steamy greenhouse or in the attic where Granny often brewed her concoctions. When the old woman had tried out new potion experiments, she had meticulously recorded everything, even her failures.

'When you learn ter see failure as a lesson, child, everything changes,' she'd told Willow once, her green hair winking in the fading daylight.

Willow had wondered at the time, considering Granny's failure had involved blowing up part of the roof, what particular lesson she had learnt. Granny had explained with a grin, *'Next time I'll try not ter blow up the roof, see?'*

Then they'd both laughed for what seemed like hours – because that wasn't a lesson Granny ever did learn.

As everyone in the tower slept on, Willow held up the tiny storm light that Holloway had given her to illuminate the notebook. It provided just enough light for her to read by, as if it could sense, somehow, exactly what she needed.

The book was bound in soft emerald-hued leather. As Willow opened it, a pale lavender alpine flower slipped out of the pages on to her lap. Willow held it up to her nose and sniffed, feeling tears edge to the corner of her eyes. It smelt faintly of beargrass, grumbling Gertrudes, cooking sherry and something that tore straight into her heart. It smelt like Granny Flossy.

She turned the pages and blinked away the film of tears, her mouth falling open in awe.

It wasn't *just* potion experiments. The book was also full of sketches – beautiful coloured drawings of plants and other things too, like what looked like a hut way up in the mountains under a blanket of snow. There were pages and pages of text, observations and memories.

Willow swallowed, poring over the notebook. Soon she was getting lost in Granny's past. Most of the early entries were about her extraordinary life in the mountains of Nach.

I arrived in the mountains during the month of Eir, the snow month. It snows most days of the year here regardless, but Eir is something else entirely. It snows as if it means it. And, if you even think of taking off a sock when not in the presence of a fire, be prepared to lose at least one of your toes. (I'm down another!)

Willow's mouth fell open. How had she not known that about Granny's toes?!

A couple of pages later, another entry caught her attention.

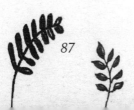

I think I've finally found a good, all-purpose potion base. It masks most of the more unpleasant flavours, while countering some of the negative side effects of many mixtures. It's a rare plant that is native to these parts, growing on the first mountain, thankfully, as I'm not sure I would have braved the shadow forest or the ice giants for it. Even so, I had one heck of a hike to get it. They are odd little purple things that grumble, reminding me of an old classmate of mine, Gertrude Kitchen. I have decided to name it after her.

Willow gasped and felt a lump in her throat. Granny had discovered and named grumbling Gertrudes! Growing up, the funny purple plants had always been a staple in the greenhouse. She blinked as a memory came floating up from a time when she was helping Granny to repot one, but it slapped her with its roots, then wriggled free.

'Ah!' Willow cried. 'These are impossible – they fight you at every turn!'

'You just need to figure out what it needs. Plants are like people: if you give them the right conditions to thrive, they can surprise you.'

She took the plant from Willow, then opened a tin box sitting on the floor. Curiously, it was full of ice. 'This is never-melt ice,' she explained, scooping some up, putting it in the bigger pot and mixing it with the soil. Then, taking the wriggling, writhing thing from Willow, she planted it inside. The grumbling Gertrude settled into the cold, icy soil with a contented sort of sigh. Granny patted it and said, 'I get grumpy when I'm hot too, mind.'

Then, to Willow's surprise, shortly afterwards, the plant started to produce a large purple fruit.

Willow smiled at the memory.

She came across more experiments and observations.

There was an accident in the hut yesterday. I was working, and Ed the yak was keeping me company while Amora suffered from one of her 'headaches'. (I must admit, I do wonder why she came to the mountains if the only work she ever planned to do was flap her lips. She complains about everything - the cold, our yak, the giants . . .)

Anyway, I was testing a new forgetfulness potion, using a flake of giant skin (Eskisor was very amenable and handed me a bit from his knee the other day when he came round for tea), but the cauldron overbubbled and exploded. It doused the yak in potion from head to hoof, and it worked - he completely forgot about me and has left the hut.

The possibilities of not only creating a forgetfulness potion but one that doesn't need to be swallowed is very intriguing . . . I wonder if this property can be applied to other potions.

(If the paper is blotchy, it's just from my

tears over missing that silly yak. Oh, how I have cried, begging him to return! But he has joined a new herd and forgotten about his time of domesticity. I am trying to resist bribing him to come back; he does seem happy in the wild.)

There was a coloured illustration of Ed the yak. He had long chestnut fur that was flecked with little green spots. Granny had written a caption that said: Ed - freckles caused by the remnants of a misfiring potion for growing year-round cabbage.

Forget Potion Recipe

1. Pulverise the skin and flesh of two fruits from a grumbling Gertrude and soak in a standard cauldron measure of cold water overnight with the juice of two lemons.

2. Add the grumbling Gertrude base to a cauldron and bring to the boil.

3. Add:

One flake of skin from a long giant's knee

A sprig of rosemary

A pinch of dried thyme

Three yak hairs

Two tears shed before a full moon.

4. Boil for seven hours. Do not let it overbubble (will explode).

5. Can be thrown on to the target rather than swallowed. As little as one ladleful can produce the desired effect. Results of forgetfulness can be unpredictable unless you announce exactly what you wish to be forgotten as you throw it.

Willow gasped softly. So that's when Granny Flossy had invented potion throws! She touched the blotchy paper, then her heart. Poor Granny! Making that potion had come at such a cost – losing her animal companion. She remembered hearing about Ed. She wondered if he ever did come back.

Willow snuggled beneath the blankets to the

faint sound of patients snoring and Daisy giving the occasional little yip in her sleep. As the night wore on and Willow kept reading, she came across potions that helped to recall memories, and ones that could change your appearance . . .

Last night, I met a living myth. She is called Walaika and haunts the first mountain during the first frost . . . a spirit who has the power to show you your worst fears being realised. Those who live out here, from giant to frost elth, leave out little talismans and tokens so that she does not enter their dwellings. They are always red. Bits of string. Mushrooms. Painted currant buns.

I was curious, so I left the door open instead.

She is tall with horns on her head, and her skin is almost transparent. I could literally see as the tea I offered her entered her ethereal body. To my surprise, she thanked me for my kindness and said that she wouldn't bring my greatest fear to life unless I wanted her to.

I thought for a while, then decided I'd like to know. She showed me an old woman who had

become so full of fear that she never left her home, never tried new things, and had stopped doing what she loved. It was HORRIFYING.

I realised then that my biggest fear is not dying or being a failure, but losing my curiosity. This is actually a relief because, well, the odds of the former are much higher!

Afterwards, Walaika said it was so rare that someone asked to see their greatest fear that she would be happy to give me another gift as well. She offered me some of her breath, which I bottled.

I tested it in a variety of recipes, but nothing seemed to happen - until I mixed it with the potion base alone and tried it. I happened to glance at myself in the mirror and nearly had a heart attack, as what was looking back at me was Walaika! Well, it turns out that her breath produces a potion that turns you into whoever you are thinking of - for about fifteen minutes . . .

Willow stared at the page in amazement. She knew her granny had always been brave and curious,

but until now she hadn't quite realised the extent. It warmed her heart to learn that yes, Granny Flossy had died, and may have been seen by some as a failure in her later years, but she never did lose her curiosity.

Willow read on with curiosity of her own, finding potions that could turn you invisible, cover someone in warts, or even make you see the fairies. (She got really excited about this one until she found that you first had to catch one and snip off some of its toenails . . .) All of them involved complicated, difficult-to-source ingredients from right across Starfell.

Leafing through the pages was like being with Granny again, the sensation warm, painful and pleasant all at the same time, like getting into a bath that is just a little too hot. Willow read all through the night, trying not to get sucked into the stories too much, forcing herself to skip ahead and skim bits, looking for a potion or a plant or *anything* that might help restore her magic.

It was hours and hours before she found something.

Near the middle of the book, at around three in the morning, Willow came across something that sparked a memory.

11

The Legend of the Winter Beast

There are over one hundred and fifty names for the different types of snow out here. Lee-flit for light snow. Fiss-lef for snow that falls to the left, and lee-flit-rih for light snow falling to the right and so on. Perhaps unsurprisingly, translation issues caused a delay in the warning that one of Eir's worst blizzards was on its way two days ago.

It was all the more unfortunate as we heard that a woman from the second mountain became stranded in the storm with her two-year-old child, and the boy, who had been born blind and deaf, died.

When the giants found them, the boy was alive, but frost-changed, his skin like snow,

his hair like ice. They say that his mother made a bargain with the mythical winter beast known as the Craegun. She gave up her magic, and in exchange the Craegun brought the boy back to life as a child of frost. He is the same boy, and still cannot see or hear, but has a unique way of communicating with his mother, drawing enchanted images and messages on her palm – remarkable in a child so young.

There is going to be a celebration later. I'm making pot roast. I cannot wait to meet this pair.

Willow stopped reading, her finger poised on the line *the mythical winter beast known as the Craegun*.

Craegun. She had heard of him before, hadn't she? But where? When?

She was exhausted. Her eyelids were growing heavy.

Memories are strange things, and they arrive at odd hours, often in that twilight space between being asleep and awake, and, while Willow mused on her

magic and the word 'Craegun', something she thought she'd forgotten hovered in her mind.

She was eight and catching glowflies in the garden. Inside the cottage, her mother was busy with a client.

Raine claimed she spoke to the dead and communicated their messages to the living, for a fee. Willow would later find out that her mother's ability was a bit hit and miss; she didn't actually get to choose which spirits came to visit her or if they spoke or not. However, she had found that her clients preferred a bit of a show, so in order to put some bread on the table she wasn't above a bit of 'poetic licence'. This often meant pretending that the ghost in the corner was a relative, or actually saying something instead of snoring or laughing at them, or even getting her two older daughters involved in the act to create some convincing special effects.

Willow caught snatches of her mother's conversation from the open window while she scooped up insects from the herm bushes beneath the windowsill. Her

ears pricked up when she heard her own name, and she released the glowflies again into the twilight air.

'I must say,' said the client, 'I was surprised to meet your youngest earlier. She's nothing like you and your other girls, is she? Same with her magic. What a pity she didn't have something more powerful like the rest of you.'

Willow sat back against the low wall, her heart sinking. Did everyone think this when they first met her?

She heard her mother say something about her taking after her father in looks. Adding, 'You know Willow's power is very handy.'

'Oh yes, I'm sure,' the client said, laughing. 'Besides, beggars can't be choosers – I mean, so many witches have children with no magic at all these days. At least she has some, even if it's just a crumb.'

Shortly afterwards, Willow's mother had told the client that the only message she was getting from beyond was that she should leave their house immediately . . .

Later that evening, the woman's words had writhed inside Willow like she'd swallowed a beehive.

99

She and Granny Flossy were inside the greenhouse when the old woman spotted her glum face.

'What's eating yer, child?'

'Nothing.'

'Tell me or I'll fill yer bed with these,' Granny teased. She was holding up yellow wriggle plants that resembled worms and liked nothing better than attaching themselves to people's toes.

Willow shuddered. Then it came out like a pot that was boiling over. 'I hate that I'm different, that I don't look like Mum and my sisters – that no one even thinks we're related! And my magic . . . Why did it have to be so weak?'

'Weak?' said Granny Flossy with great surprise. Willow nodded.

'It ain't weak, child, it's growing, like you. It's the kind of skill that doesn't announce itself with bells, sure, but fool's gold often glitters much brighter than the real thing. Ye've got ter look properly ter see its real value.'

Willow looked confused and Granny explained. 'Your magic isn't weak. In fact, it bears a similarity to the legendary Craegun – a beast who lives deep within the seven mountains of Nach. The story goes

that he slumbers for all time, only to awaken when he encounters a worthy soul. He can restore what someone has lost – anything at all, from lost fortunes to loved ones – but for a heavy price . . . Think o' that. And people pay it, risking life and limb to be near his magic. And look at you! You offer something so similar, even if it's on a smaller scale.'

Willow sat up with a jolt.

The Craegun . . . The legendary beast who had a magical ability like her own, just far, far more powerful. Granny had made it sound as if it could restore anything . . .

Anything at all.

What about *lost magic*?

Willow's heart thundered. How had she forgotten this story?

She stared at the notebook, then shook her head. Maybe she hadn't forgotten about the Craegun, not really. In some odd way, her brain had been trying to remember, hadn't it? Wasn't this the reason she was

convinced, without really knowing why, that Granny Flossy would have the answer? Because a part of her *knew* she'd heard this story once before, and she just needed reminding?

She closed the book, then blinked as something else occurred to her. Was *this* who Amora Spell had meant when she'd goaded Willow earlier? As Granny's former potions partner, she would have heard the legend too!

'I would 'ave thought that you'd be in the mountains, trying ter find that beast, trying ter get yer magic back . . .'

Willow had thought she was referring to *Silas*, that he was the 'beast' imprisoned by the rock dragons in the Cloud Mountains with the elf staff that contained her magic.

But Amora wasn't speaking about Silas at all, was she? She was talking about a real beast. The Craegun.

And now Willow knew just what she had to do.

12

The Spirit Hare

A dark fog seeped beneath the front door, billowing upwards as it climbed the stairs and made itself at home.

Willow awoke with a start to the sound of anxious barking. She must have fallen asleep. The noise had come from Daisy, Willow's roommate, whose hackles were raised as she barked wildly, standing on the end of her bed, her eyes glued to the door.

Oswin was wide awake and shaking too. '**Oh no, oh, me g r e e d y aunt,**' he breathed, dashing into Willow's arms. '**What new eel is this?**'

In the darkness, they could see a mist creeping into their room, slithering beneath the door. Willow felt her spine turn to glass.

There were shouts and screams from the other

patients and the sound of doors opening and closing, then the frantic shuffle of feet on the stairwell.

'What *is* this?' Willow whispered. She grabbed her storm light and searched inwards for her courage, then edged forward, one step at a time. She breathed slightly more easily as the encroaching fog seemed to slink away from the light's beam. Oswin jumped out of her arms, and he and Daisy followed close behind as Willow opened the door and peered out.

The hallway was completely shrouded in fog, but the storm light helped them to see, causing the fog to recoil slightly from its glow. Willow crept out to join the worried patients on the landing, scanning through the shifting haze for a glimpse of Essential.

Then there was a knock on the tower door.

Followed by another.

Willow peered down the stairs in fright. There was a familiar *clink-clank-clink*, and Pimpernell appeared through the mist, heading to the door.

There, surrounded by fog, was Moreg Vaine. She stood in the doorway like a candle in the dark, her eyes like gimlets.

Willow's relief at the sight of the familiar witch was short-lived.

'It is what we feared,' said Moreg. 'Silas is on the move.'

'**Oh, me 'orrid aunt Osbertrude,**' breathed Oswin, and Willow's breath caught in her throat.

Pimpernell nodded, her silvery dreadlocks shining in the dim glow from the storm light. She turned to glance at Willow on the stairs, her amber eyes like wood snapping in a fire, then looked back at the visiting witch. 'Is he after Willow?'

'He may be, but for now he has been prevented from locating her.'

Willow felt her knees buckle slightly in relief, and she had to reach out for the bannister to steady herself.

'Thankfully, the wispdust has kept her shrouded, and I have used this Flummox Fog on my journey here to travel undetected.'

'Where is he now?' breathed Willow, descending the stairs slowly. The patients on either side made room, squeezing themselves tightly to the rails. 'What is he doing?'

Moreg held up a finger, then turned. She seemed to hold the gaze of something outside for a moment, then she nodded, as if satisfied, before stepping inside the tower. Just as the door closed, Willow thought she spotted a pale rabbit or hare, which darted out of sight.

Moreg raised her palms, and the fog inside the tower began to dissipate. This caused a hubbub from

several patients.

'Oh Wol, is that *the* Moreg Vaine?'

'Did she just make that fog disappear?'

'Is she taking us all to Netherfell? They say she has tea parties with the dead.'

'Does she think that will keep us safe from Silas?'

'I heard she pickles people in vinegar – who's ter say she's helping us? Maybe she's conspiring with Silas.'

'She can hear what you're thinking! Oh Wol . . .'

Pimpernell turned

to face them. 'Back ter yer beds, please!'

No one moved. Pimpernell tapped her cane, and her eyes seemed to snap fire. 'I shall not repeat meself.'

Still they lingered nervously. Moreg turned to the patients and sighed, like she was praying for strength. 'I am not whisking you to the realm of the undead. I cannot read minds, nor do I pickle people in vinegar . . .' Then she gave a wry sort of grin. 'Usually, it's ginger . . .'

'**I knew** it!' breathed Oswin.

'I meant the *rumour* is usually ginger,' said Moreg.

'**Oh,**' said Oswin, sounding a little disappointed.

Moreg sighed. 'I know Silas breaking out is a concern for all of us – but I can assure you that you have nothing to fear from me. I want to prevent him endangering anyone, and as such this is an Enchancil issue now.'

'Which means it's not fer yer ears,' said Pimpernell. ''Sides, if we need to confront him, the best thing you lot can do ter be in with a fighting chance is get yer rest first.'

They still hesitated, and Pimpernell's patience officially ran out. She tapped her cane on the floor and hissed, 'Did I not make meself clear? Back ter yer

beds! The difference between Moreg and I is that the things yeh've heard about me are *not* rumours.'

Willow heard someone behind her gulp loudly. She didn't blame them. Soon everyone was hurrying back to their rooms.

Willow wasn't one of them. Neither was Essential, who had appeared behind her. Their gazes were fixed on the older witches.

'I want to know what's going on,' repeated Willow.

'Me too,' said Essential.

Because of their age, Willow and Essential were not technically Enchancil members, but, given that they had both *fought* Silas before, Moreg – like Rubix – kept them informed.

Moreg and Pimpernell nodded.

'Come ter me study,' said Pimpernell, pointing to a room next to the kitchen.

Pimpernell's study was a small, handsome room complete with wall-to-ceiling bookshelves, a cheery fire crackling in the fireplace, two armchairs and a green velvet sofa.

'Take a seat,' said Pimpernell, but Willow was too agitated to sit down.

Just then, a whistling sound came from somewhere.

Moreg patted her cloak. 'Where did I put it?'
She reached deep inside her pocket, her arm almost
disappearing, and took out a copper teakettle, as if
that were a perfectly ordinary thing to do. She then
stood up to hang it off a hook in the fireplace.

Willow, desperate to hear news of Silas, didn't feel
now was the time for tea – but she soon saw that this
was not what Moreg's kettle was for at all. Steam began
to fill the room, rising from the shiny copper spout,
and above their heads it formed into fat, loopy words.

*Moss family safe with me.
Silas not seen.*

'**Wot the—?**' cried Oswin.

'It's a message from Rubix,'
Moreg explained.

'Thank Starfell fer that at
least,' muttered Pimpernell.

The ground seemed for
a moment to shift beneath
Willow's feet. Relief flooded
her senses. Silas hadn't got to
her family.

'How does this work?' asked Essential, inspecting the steam, her glasses fogging up.

'Kettle charm,' explained Moreg, showing her the complicated spout that had several levers. 'Rubix and Holloway made them for some of the key members of the Enchancil because raven messages could get intercepted – not to mention how long they take to deliver. With the way things are heading . . . well, we thought a method of sending messages faster was a good idea.'

'At least everyone's safe for now,' said Willow.

Moreg shook her head. 'I'm afraid not. It's time I told you, Willow, that Silas has been free of the rock dragons for some weeks.'

Willow gasped. 'What do you mean?'

'I was able to keep tabs on his whereabouts thanks to a trusted source, and to learn that you were not in immediate danger, but it seems new plans are in motion.'

Essential looked incensed. 'You knew he was free of the rock dragons all this time and you didn't tell us?'

'Moreg, what are you talking about?' cried Willow.

'I can understand your frustration, and of all

people, Willow, considering everything that you have faced with Silas and the fact that he is after the iron half-moon, you have a right to know. But the situation has been very precarious. As you're aware, not so long ago the Enchancil was infiltrated and its members manipulated by Gerful chalk – we could not take that chance again.'

'We?' asked Willow.

'Pimpernell – as your trusted guardian at present – is the only other member who knew the truth.'

There was a faint warbling call, the kind a woodland bird might make, from outside.

Moreg held up a finger, asking the others to wait. The warbling continued. Moreg nodded, then she made the same warbling sound.

A second later, to Willow's amazement, a hare appeared. It walked through the walls of the tower as if they were nothing more than air, and came to rest near Moreg's heels. Willow did a double take. It was glowing faintly blue, like a ghost. She blinked at it in shock.

'There you are,' said Moreg. 'He's not following?'

The hare shook its head, and Moreg looked relieved. They all stared at it curiously.

'Is – is that hare . . . a *ghost?*' whispered Essential.

'Wot is 'appening?' breathed Oswin.

'Ah,' said Moreg. 'Allow me to introduce my sister, Molsa.'

13

Molsa's Tale

'Molsa?' cried Willow. 'Your dead sister, Molsa? As in . . . Silas's mother?'

'Yes.'

Willow stared in disbelief. 'But—'

'I was shocked too, child,' said Pimpernell with a nod.

'I know,' said Moreg, well aware of their confusion and amazement. 'It's a bit of a long story, but I'll try to keep it brief. You see, when we left Netherfell on the *Sudsfarer* last year, unbeknown to any of us, we had a stowaway – Molsa.'

Willow exchanged glances with Essential. The idea that they'd had a secret ghostly passenger was unnerving to say the least.

Moreg continued. 'Afterwards, I began to suspect

that I was being watched and followed, and I waited. Eventually, Molsa revealed herself. She was angry with me, understandably, so it has taken a long time to regain her trust.'

'Regain her trust?' echoed Willow.

Molsa herself nodded in response, and then, before their eyes, she transformed. She grew from a hare into a ghostly woman with long dark hair and dark eyes – eyes that looked desperately sad.

'You see, I was a lost soul, trapped in the realm of the undead alongside all those others with unfinished business. A part of me couldn't move on to my final resting place.

'When I passed, I'd just had a baby, and I longed for news about him.

'Then, suddenly, you and Moreg arrived in Netherfell, and I heard about the welfare of my son at last. But it was like a nightmare – nothing as I had hoped. I discovered that my sister had not raised Silas, but given him away. Instead, he'd been brought up by the man I'd mistakenly fallen for and taught to despise the very part of himself that made him unique – taught to hate that he was magic.' Molsa looked pained. 'Suddenly it was as if I was given life, but it was a half-life, filled with rage and torment that clouded everything. I didn't see past my own sense of betrayal. I did what I could to escape Netherfell. I wanted desperately to find my son, to help him. And, yes, to get my revenge on Moreg for causing him – and me – this pain.'

Willow felt her throat constrict. She couldn't help feeling sorry for Molsa.

Moreg explained. 'It was Molsa who stole Holloway's clouded eye from Rubix – preventing me from seeing what Silas planned.'

'**Wot?**' said Oswin, his eyes bulging.

He wasn't the only one to gasp in horror. Willow's pity fused with anger.

'But in getting your revenge on Moreg you helped him get the elf staff,' said Willow.

'You put everyone's lives at risk!'

Molsa closed her eyes and nodded. She seemed racked by torment.

'I-I didn't see for a long time how poisoned he was, or the true cost of his plans. I thought if he became powerful he would give the Brothers of Wol magic too, and that he'd see that he wasn't born wrong . . . I thought that, given time, his plans might change, soften, with me by his side – someone to love and support him.'

Willow heard the pain in her voice and felt another rising swell of pity battle with her frustration.

'But eventually I saw how deeply ingrained his hatred of magic had become. Instead of seeing it as a gift and using it to change the Brothers of Wol from the inside – making them understand that those with magic aren't impure or evil – it was like he wanted to change *himself* to become more acceptable to them, even now.

'He believes that he is making himself into a god, and that, when he does, everything will be better. I tried to stop him, to reason with him. I was angry

with my sister, but I've realised that she, in her own way, thought the same thing I did – that there was hope for Silas, and that the Brothers of Wol could change. But, of course, that didn't happen.'

Moreg looked at her sister. 'Molsa, if I could go back and do things differently, I would. I hope you know that. It is one of my greatest regrets.'

Molsa inclined her head. 'I know. It took me a long time to accept your apology. I think, had I not experienced the same wishful thinking myself, I might never have understood.'

The sisters shared a solemn look of understanding.

'But where is Silas now?' asked Essential, her eyes wide. 'Why did the rock dragons think he was still with them?'

Willow nodded – it was a good question.

Molsa turned back to them. 'When Silas escaped the rock dragons, he used some illusion magic to fool them into believing that he was still there for weeks. He returned to Wolkana in secret, and I was given instructions to locate Willow.'

Willow blinked. 'You were?'

She nodded. 'When Silas failed to find you using magic, I tracked you to your cottage in Grinfog. I

118

found you early one morning, outside in the garden, trying to mount your broom and failing . . . There was a blanket round your shoulders. Your face looked tired and pale – you were obviously very ill.'

Willow swallowed. She'd never for a moment imagined anyone had witnessed her attempts to fly her broom.

'Oh, Willow,' said Essential softly.

'I saw the true cost of my revenge,' continued Molsa. 'By preventing Moreg from seeing Silas's plans, I had caused this – an innocent young girl was tricked into unleashing the elf staff, only to have her magic stolen from her. Shame flooded me. I knew then that Silas had to be stopped, that he couldn't be allowed to take anyone else's magic. I realised I had to bury my own pain and anger, and so I approached Moreg.'

Willow was floored.

Moreg surreptitiously wiped her eyes with the corner of a handkerchief and nodded. 'Until then, we hadn't wanted to disrupt your life any more than necessary, Willow, but this was a painful lesson that the wispdust alone was not enough. I spoke to your mother, and we moved you here to keep you safe and your family to Rubix's.'

119

Molsa nodded. 'Silas had already predicted that you might have been hidden, so when I came back, saying that I couldn't find you, he told me to keep trying. I said I would. While I don't believe that Silas is aware that I am working with Moreg, my attempts to change his mind mean that he knows I don't fully support his decisions any more. I think this is why he hasn't been keeping me as informed recently. He's been careful to keep the specific details of his plans private, so there is much I do not know. I'm trying to glean as much as I can.'

Willow frowned, her head spinning. She'd heard everything Molsa had said, and she felt incredibly moved. She understood, perhaps better than some, how guilt could eat you from the inside. She wanted to believe that Molsa had joined them . . . but how many times had she fallen for someone's tricks? In her heart, she wanted, *needed* to trust what Molsa said, but what if she were wrong in doing so? What if Molsa were planning to rush back and tell Silas what *they* were planning? So much was at stake – if Silas succeeded, it could rip their world apart. She had to be strong, if not for herself then for Starfell. Could they really trust Molsa? Willow felt like she needed something more tangible than words as proof. Starfell deserved that.

'Molsa, I'm sure you can understand – I need to know that you've really joined us. Can't you do something to truly stop Silas? You could steal the clouded eye back so Moreg can see what he's up to! Or steal the *staff* even—'

Molsa looked stricken. 'I can't, Willow. I'm really sorry. I understand how you must feel, and I assure you I want to do more but I can't risk Silas doubting my loyalties. He doesn't let the staff or the eye out of his sight. One wrong move and it could all be over . . .'

Moreg nodded. 'She's right. If he suspects Molsa, our only source of intelligence about him will be jeopardised. Not to mention that if he feels that he's been betrayed he could become even more vindictive, even more reckless. For now, as far as we can tell, he hasn't acted rashly, and we need to keep it that way.'

Willow nodded reluctantly. She didn't want to think about how much worse it could be if Silas thought he were backed into a corner.

'But, Moreg . . . I know she's your sister, but are you *sure* we can trust her?' Essential pressed, adding awkwardly, 'Um, sorry, Molsa.'

'I am,' said Moreg, looking as serious as Willow had ever seen her.

Pimpernell had been quiet for a while, her eyes narrowed. 'I believe it too.'

Willow looked at the hedge witch. 'What makes you so sure?'

Pimpernell's eyes flashed, and she said something Willow had heard many times before: 'Pimpernell always knows, child.'

'**I is detectin' no lies** meself,' Oswin admitted.

Willow looked at him gratefully. As a kobold, Oswin could sense when someone was being dishonest – and Willow had to admit it was true that Pimpernell had a spooky ability to know things too. When they'd first met, she'd identified Willow's magic ability without ever being told of it. Perhaps they *could* trust Molsa.

'All right,' said Willow, feeling relieved. 'So, what is Silas up to now?'

Moreg looked at them. 'We don't know much, but we do know he's now preparing for the next stage of his plan.'

Molsa nodded. 'First he wanted to search for you and the iron half-moon, Willow, but now there's something else as well.'

'What?' breathed Willow.

'He has been working on an alternative plan . . . a way to repair the elf staff.'

'A way to *repair* it?' Essential echoed.

'But how?' asked Willow.

'I don't know yet,' Molsa confessed. 'Like I said, he has been careful not to reveal the details to me. But I know he just left Wolkana for the first time since his return, to act on his new plan.'

Moreg's eyes turned white momentarily. 'I believe that very shortly we will receive news that may enlighten us.'

14

News from Wisperia

The raven Willow had used to send her message to Nolin Sometimes arrived, flying through the window in the tower's attic that was left open especially for him. Willow, Essential, Pimpernell and Moreg were waiting for him in anticipation, and Frank came in to land on Pimpernell's outstretched hand with a letter in his claws.

Pimpernell opened it.

'It's addressed ter me – and you, Willow,' she said, clutching her chest.

Willow came forward to peer over the woman's shoulder, blanching at the first line of the letter and looking up at Moreg in horror.

'You're right.'

'What is it?' asked Essential.

124

'It's from Sometimes.'

Dear Willow and Pimpernell,

Beroc, my friend, was captured and tortured by Silas. He managed to escape and find me in my house at the top of the Great Wisperia Tree. I've tried all my own remedies, but nothing is working. It's not clear if he will survive much longer without help. Pimpernell, can you come quickly?

He says that he needs to stay alive long enough to tell you something, Willow — something important. He won't tell me what it is, in case the message gets intercepted. Please come soon.

Nolin Sometimes

PS Willow, I'm afraid the phenomenon that you described in your letter is possibly worse than you realise. If you come, I will explain more.

125

Willow gasped. The scroll slipped from her fingers and Essential used her powers to freeze it, then plucked it from mid-air to read.

'Beroc,' said Essential, pushing her glasses back up her nose. 'That name sounds familiar.'

'**Yep,**' said Oswin. Willow hadn't seen him follow them upstairs from the study. He sat by Willow's feet. "E wos the one **wiff** the green **flames** coming out of 'is 'ead. I remembers it **well** cos 'e wos the one giving the **orders** when they *captured us*.'

It was true. Beroc was one of the forest people of Wisperia who had captured them a while ago, when they believed Willow and her friends were involved with Nolin Sometimes's disappearance. They'd let them go when Beroc and his tribe realised they were all on the same side. They'd even given Willow a ferili seed from the Great Wisperia Tree that ended up helping them when they finally found Sometimes in Netherfell.

'Did you know about this – about Beroc?' asked Willow, whirling round to confront Molsa.

'No!' Molsa looked horrified. 'I did suspect something was happening in the dungeon, and I attempted to follow to find out – but it was guarded.

When I made to enter, three of Silas's men told me that it didn't concern me. I waited till they were asleep and tried to slip through the walls, but something prevented me. I believe Silas has used the staff's magic to ensure that I cannot go where he doesn't want me to be. But, even then, I never suspected this – a man tortured . . .'

There was a heavy silence at that. They all looked stricken.

'I wonder what Beroc needs to tell me,' Willow said, worried.

'I wish I could just *see* what it is,' said Moreg, touching her head in frustration, 'but, because it's all wrapped up with Silas and he still has the clouded eye, I can't. I have this feeling we're missing something vital.'

Willow blinked. That didn't seem good at all.

The old clock in the hallway chimed the hour: it was five in the morning. Willow was far too agitated for sleep, and this didn't sound like something that could wait.

Moreg seemed to be thinking the same thing. 'We need to go, and now.'

'Essential, help me gather as many of me remedies as we can carry,' said Pimpernell.

127

Molsa looked at them. 'I need to return to Wolkana. He cannot know I was here.'

They watched as she turned once more into a hare and darted out of sight.

The Great Wisperia Tree dominated the forest, with its pale blue bark, the colour of sea glass. The air was still as they made their way to Nolin Sometimes's treehouse at the top, under a canopy of stars. The suspended rocks that formed a flight of stairs lit up one by one as they flew, landing on the porch.

Pimpernell propped the Ambulbroom against the railing, where Sometimes was waiting for them. His all-white hair stood out in a cloud around his head, and his young face looked tired and worried, yet relieved at the sight of them. He rushed forward to greet them, only to frown and stop dead in his tracks.

'Great Starfell!' he cried. Then his eyes turned completely white and he crashed over in a dead faint.

'Oh no,' said Willow. 'It's the memories washing over him!'

As a forgotten teller, Sometimes couldn't help but see the memories of the people near him. He could even connect to the consciousness of plants and

other forms of nature too. Unfortunately, when he experienced these visions, he often collapsed – which was why he lived in such an isolated spot.

''Ow **many** times 'ave I said livin' on **top** of this **tree** is jes not a **good idea** fer this gizard?' muttered Oswin, his paws covering his eyes, while Willow, Moreg and Essential hurried to pick him up.

Sometimes mumbled incoherently as they carried him into the house.

Immediately, their attention turned to the faint cries coming from the person in Sometimes's bed. It was the flame-haired man, Beroc, although the flames had been extinguished, and he looked wan and shivery, clutching his sides.

Pimpernell rushed over to examine him. 'Tell me wot happened to yeh, Beroc!'

But the man grabbed hold of her hand for a moment. 'Willow . . . I must speak to Willow. It's urgent.'

Willow left Moreg and Essential to settle Sometimes on the sofa and came to stand beside Beroc. 'I'm here.'

'It *is* you,' he said, relieved.

Willow nodded. 'Sometimes said you wanted to speak with me, that you escaped so that you could . . . Why?'

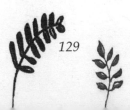

He closed his eyes and nodded, letting go of Pimpernell's hand. 'As you know, those of us who are native to Wisperia speak Liral, the first language. We are the last community in Starfell to do so. Silas captured me because he wanted someone to translate this,' he said. He shifted uncomfortably, wincing, and took something out of an inside pocket in his leather vest. It was a rolled-up scroll, which he held out to Willow.

She took it, confused, and stared at the paper. It was written in a language she didn't recognise and seemed very old. At first, she didn't understand, and then, finally, *she did.*

'This is the scroll that Silas stole from Library – the ancient elvish scroll that was supposed to contain the location of the vanished kingdom . . . But how . . . how could you decode it?' Willow frowned, remembering what she had learnt about the scroll from the rock dragons. 'I thought only elves of Queen Almefeira's bloodline would be able to.'

'Yes,' said Beroc. 'Elves were the first people. Many of us in the ancient community of Wisperia are descendants of elves, some of us even of the queen's line.'

Willow still didn't understand. 'But what use is this scroll to Silas now? I already brought Llandunia back.' She felt a familiar pang of regret.

Beroc winced with pain from his wounds. 'The whereabouts of the kingdom is not all the scroll contains. It tells of something far worse.'

Moreg and Essential stepped closer to listen. The air suddenly felt charged as they waited for him to explain.

'It contains the story of *how the elf staff was made.'*

'**Oh, me greedy aunt!**' gasped Oswin.

Moreg and Willow glanced at each other in horror.

'Silas made me translate it against my will, by spreading Gerful chalk on my skin.'

Pimpernell gasped. 'No!'

Willow frowned. She knew that Gerful chalk could be used to brainwash and manipulate people – it happened to so many of her friends and family when Silas was rounding up magical children. As far as she knew, the chalk was used on walls and floors, areas people would pass through, leaving their minds in a receptive state. She had never heard of it being applied directly to someone's body.

Oswin turned pale, and he was the one to explain. '**Gerful chalks is powerful, so powerful that yew on'y needs ter steps overs it fer it ter work. Puttings it on yer skins or furs is unforgivables. It would** *burn*, **forcing someones ter do wot yer want on'y cos they is in such pain.**'

Essential and Willow shared looks of horror.

Pimpernell had already snapped into action, rummaging in her bag of ingredients and hurrying

over to Sometimes's kitchen to prepare remedies.

Beroc nodded. 'Silas didn't care. He knew that I was fighting him, fighting the chalk that was spread on the ground, so he took it to extremes . . . After that, I was unable to resist. I just wish that I had been able to stop myself.' He looked racked with guilt. 'I told him what it said . . . how the elf staff was created . . .'

Willow swallowed, remembering what Molsa had warned them about. 'He – he knows how to repair the staff?'

Beroc nodded. 'He just needs to create a new iron half-moon. And he can do this by using the blood of Queen Almefeira's direct heir, from the matriarchal line.'

Willow looked from Moreg to Beroc, the colour draining from her face. 'What?'

Beroc's face crumpled. 'He spoke of an elvish girl. Apparently, she is the one who would inherit the staff – the girl who controls the north wind . . .'

'Twist!' cried Willow, her heart in her throat. There was a rushing sound of blood in her ears, and spots before her eyes.

'**Oh no!**' gasped Oswin.

Essential clamped a hand over her mouth in fright.

133

'Yes,' said Beroc. 'On my way here, I tried to send warning to Lael, but my message may have been intercepted – or it may not have made it to the family in time. I needed to tell you, Willow, because you're the one who has stopped Silas in the past. Magic put its faith in you once before. All the forest people felt it.'

Willow stood up fast, barely able to process this information. 'We need to find her! Protect her!'

Moreg's face had turned white.

'The ritual to create the new iron half-moon using the elvish girl's blood can only occur during the greening moons, when spring finally arrives – that's in four days' time,' said Beroc. 'You have till then to try and stop him.'

'I have to go – I need to get to Twist!' cried Willow, panicking.

But Moreg shook her head. Her eyes, pinned somewhere in the distance, turned white.

'It's too late.'

15

The Great Wisperia Tree

'T-too late?' breathed Willow.

Moreg nodded, her eyes still white. She put a hand on the wall to steady herself. 'She's been taken.'

Essential came forward, steering Moreg towards a seat.

Willow stood rooted to the spot. He had taken Twist. Her friend. All she could think of was what Beroc had said just seconds ago. *Blood.* Silas would need her *blood.*

'Is . . . is she alive?'

It was Beroc who answered. 'He won't kill her – the blood needs to be fresh for the ritual.'

Willow bent over, struggling to catch a breath. Panic was causing spots to swarm before her eyes. She thought she might be sick.

She looked up. Pimpernell was carrying a freshly prepared salve to Beroc's bedside, and Moreg and Essential were sitting in shock on the sofa beside Sometimes, who was still fading in and out of consciousness as he caught up on their memories. No one was preparing to leave.

Tears threatened. 'We need to go after her!'

'We can't,' said Moreg. She looked utterly despondent.

Willow felt like screaming. Moreg, so powerful, so revered, had never seemed more fragile, or more human, than right then, when Willow needed her more than she ever had before.

'He'll have taken her back to Wolkana,' Moreg continued, her voice hollow.

'So then we need a dragon or a troll to get inside, like last time,' said Willow.

The fortress of the Brothers of Wol was heavily guarded, and its magical protection ensured that no witch or wizard could gain entry, unless they were escorted by one of the Brothers – but Silas hadn't factored in other magical creatures.

Pimpernell looked up from treating Beroc. 'He has learnt from this mistake, child. He is many things, but not a fool.'

136

'The Enchancil has been trying for weeks to breach Wolkana, to convince the rest of the Brothers to join us,' Moreg reminded Willow. 'The protection has been reinforced to block magical creatures too. Feathering and Calamity have both tried and failed to enter. There's no way in.'

Tears began to slip down Willow's face. She felt utterly helpless, and it angered her. 'But we can't just do nothing, Moreg! How could you not have seen . . . *something*? Anything?' she yelled. 'You put all these measures in place to protect me, but now poor Twist . . .'

Moreg looked wretched. 'I know.'

As soon as the outburst had come swarming from Willow's lips, like bees ready to sting, she regretted it instantly. Silas had been very careful to ensure that any of Moreg's visions concerning him were blocked by the clouded eye. Even from their very first encounter, he had admitted that Moreg was the one person he knew could stop him, and that was why he worked so hard to make sure she couldn't see his plans.

'I'm so sorry,' said Willow. She understood, more than most, how horrible it was to feel consumed

137

by guilt. For a moment, she was reminded of poor Holloway and all those *shoulds* he couldn't control. She didn't want to put that on Moreg. 'You couldn't have known – he made sure of that.'

Moreg nodded, but her face looked racked with guilt regardless. 'Perhaps I should have pushed Molsa harder . . . Perhaps I should have encouraged her to steal back the eye after all . . .'

Willow bit her lip. It was unsettling to see the powerful witch doubt herself. 'But, like you both said back at the tower, she would probably have been caught, and he would have just sped up his plans.'

Essential sighed. 'There's no use looking back. We have to look ahead, don't we? There has to be *something* we can do.'

Moreg paused. 'We have time, but we will need to think and plan our next move very carefully.' Then she went to sit in the kitchen. It was clear she wanted a moment to herself to do just that.

As the morning progressed, Pimpernell looked after Beroc, and Sometimes finally came round. Essential made tea, rummaged around for some breakfast and started preparing food for them all.

Every part of Willow wanted – needed – some kind of a plan. Not this. Not this quiet, domestic scene. These ordinary, everyday things made her feel a bit like screaming. They had four days!

That was it. Four days to come up with a plan to save Twist.

She slipped outside in the early-morning light, went to sit on a wide branch of the Great Wisperia Tree and sighed. She felt exhausted and in desperate need of sleep, but she knew she wouldn't be able to rest.

There had to be a way to get inside the fortress.

There *had* to be a way to save Twist.

The idea of her fierce, wonderful friend – who tamed the north wind and had wild, electrified hair, who made thunder and lightning erupt from her mouth, who brimmed with confidence and gave the best presents – captured, frightened and alone made Willow feel *ill*.

She wanted to tear Silas apart for it.

She was a storm of emotions – angry, sad, lost and helpless. She knew that no one was to blame except Silas, but she wanted to scream at the injustice of it all. How could Moreg not have seen *anything* – even

a tiny glimpse of this? How could the Enchancil not have found out? How could the elves not have realised something like this might happen? Why did the ancient elvish queen write that scroll? How had the rock dragons not realised they'd lost their prisoner?

How had she put them all in this situation in the first place by bringing the elf staff back into the world? The guilt washed over Willow like a tide.

She sighed, closing her eyes, and leant back against the trunk of the Great Wisperia Tree. Once again, her mind was full of would-haves, could-haves and should-haves.

She felt the Great Tree flinch softly beneath her. She opened her eyes, only to blink in shock. In the growing light, she could see that it was . . . *sick.*

She swallowed. There were still parts that were sea green, but large patches had become dull and grey, and it was covered in black spots, like some of the other trees she'd seen. The branches, which usually grew the most delightful and strange creations, from apple-pie blossom to jam-tart leaves, were bare, the leaves wilted and brown.

Willow touched it softly, tears pricking her eyes as

she whispered, 'What's happening to you?'

To her surprise, Sometimes answered. He'd come to stand behind her so quietly she hadn't even heard. 'It's dying, Willow,' he said, caressing the bark like he would the hand of an ailing friend.

Willow felt her heart catch in her throat. 'Dying?' she breathed. She didn't know how she could take any more bad news.

He nodded and tears slipped down his nose. He took a seat next to her. 'I noticed it growing sick a few weeks ago. I've tried everything I can think of to help it.'

Willow wiped her eyes. 'I've seen other trees affected like this too,' she said. 'The ones I wrote to you about.'

He nodded. 'Like I said, it's worse than you feared. It's spreading rapidly among trees and flowers. I believe it is affecting other things in different ways too.'

Willow thought of all the odd sights she'd noticed herself. The Midnight Market, and the strange darkness that covered it – the black scars on the countryside as well. Then she thought back to the bark berries she'd had the day before, and how Holloway had spoken of the water from the Knotweed River tasting . . . odd.

She felt a shiver run through her because, before

141

Sometimes said what he thought, she was beginning to suspect it.

'I think it's because of Silas,' he said.

Willow swallowed.

'Whatever he's doing with the elf staff – it's affecting magic,' Sometimes went on. 'The magic of Starfell. It's what runs through all the trees, down their roots and into the earth. It's what connects us all.'

Willow's throat started to turn dry. 'What's happening to it?'

'It is ailing. If the world stays as it is, it could die.'

'B-but why?'

'I think Silas has upset the balance somehow. No one is supposed to hold so much power and, by hoarding it, reinforcing Wolkana and increasing his power, he is beginning to rip magic away even without the iron half-moon, because it has to come from somewhere – and that's all around us.'

Willow blinked. She felt the tears begin to leak down her face. 'This is happening because I brought the staff back from underground. The ancient queen knew how dangerous it was.' She touched the tree again. 'I wish I could undo what I did,' she whispered.

A snowflake fell from the sky and landed on her head. Followed by another, and another. Willow blinked back her tears and held out a hand.

'What is happening?' she cried, remembering the random snowflakes she had seen the day before too.

It was beautiful – a small, perfect flurry of snow, falling just over them.

Sometimes held his palm out to catch a snowflake of his own. For a moment, his eyes turned white, then they returned to blue, and he looked at Willow in wonder. 'It's trying to tell you something.'

'What is?' Willow asked.

Sometimes smiled. 'Magic itself.'

'Magic?' Willow frowned. The snowflakes. They had happened every time she'd noticed the black spots on the trees. 'Magic is trying to tell me something? What?'

Sometimes's eyes turned white, and he collapsed into a faint. Panicking, Willow scrambled to catch him – but he was behind her, and she didn't get there in time. His fingers slipped from her grasp, and she watched helplessly as he tumbled from the branch.

'*No!*' she cried, her heart roaring in her ears.

143

But then, almost immediately, she saw movement below. She watched in awe as the Great Wisperia Tree moved to catch Sometimes and cradle him gently in one of its branches.

Willow fell to her knees with relief, and suddenly the tears were falling hard and fast.

The two were connected, she realised. The tree responded to Sometimes, just like the forgotten teller did to it. All these years, he had never been in danger of falling.

Sometimes opened his eyes, as calm as if nothing had happened.

Willow sat on her haunches, peering down at him in the foliage below.

'It said you know what to do already,' said Sometimes.
'Who you need to find.'

Before he added anything more, it dawned on her.

'The Craegun,' Willow whispered.

16

Magic's Request

'I have a plan,' said Willow, coming into the kitchen and finding Moreg and Essential still sitting next to each other, their untouched cups of tea in front of them.

Despite their exhaustion, they both sat up straight. Even Oswin, who had fallen asleep beneath the table, crept out to listen. In the back corner of the treehouse, Pimpernell and Beroc were talking quietly, and Sometimes had gone over to help.

'I think I know a way I can get my magic back and get the elf staff away from Silas.'

Moreg looked at Willow quizzically, and then her eyes turned white for a moment as she experienced a vision. 'I see mountains and snow.'

From above Willow's head, another small flurry of

snowflakes fell from nowhere.

'**Wot the—?**' cried Oswin.

Willow caught one in her palm. 'Magic has been trying to show me what to do.'

Moreg blinked, then looked at Willow. 'You said you know a way to get your magic back . . . ? You can't mean . . . the Craegun?' she guessed, her face turning white.

Willow nodded.

'**Wot are yew on abouts?**' asked Oswin, who had come to stand by Willow's feet.

'Long ago, Granny Flossy told me about a creature that lived in the mountains of Nach – a great beast who is said to restore anything that is lost, known as the Craegun. I had forgotten about it, but when my magic was taken from me I had this *feeling* that Granny Flossy might have the answer. With Essential's help, we managed to get hold of her old notebook, and as I was reading it last night I came across the story again. I realised I already knew it. I think, in a weird way, my brain was trying to remind me of it – and, as spooky as it sounds, I think *Magic* wanted to remind me too.'

147

'Remind you of what – this Craegun?' asked Essential.

Willow nodded. 'If I can persuade him to restore my magic, I might be able to get the elf staff back. Without the staff itself, Silas would have no need for Twist. Hopefully, we could find a way to help her escape. It's not a perfect plan, I know, but—'

'But how would you be able to get the elf staff?' asked Moreg. 'It's in the fortress, so it is protected. The entire Enchancil have attempted to breach it with their powerful, combined magic, to no avail.'

Willow slipped her hand inside her pocket and brought out the missing piece of the elf staff, shaped like a half-moon. She looked at Moreg, then at the others. 'Because I won't need to get inside. I'll just need to lure him *out* – with this. I think he'll still want it because it's easier and faster than performing a ritual. I can ask for an exchange: Twist for the iron half-moon. If I'm successful with the Craegun, I will have my magic back, but he won't know that – and I can then use it to get the staff away from him.'

Essential stood up fast. She looked excited. 'That could actually work!'

Willow looked at her. 'Um, thanks,' she said.

'Sorry, I didn't mean to sound surprised. I just

mean it's simple but effective – he wouldn't dream that you would have your magic back. Also, you're like a loose thread to him, and he'd want to see that tied up – I think he'd definitely come out to see you. And, by getting him to bring Twist as the exchange, we'd be able to rescue her without breaking into the fortress. Only . . . is there a chance he's used something like wispdust to protect the staff, even outside the fortress?'

Moreg looked thoughtful 'The information I have from Molsa is that all of Silas's efforts at this stage have been to protect the fortress itself. From the start, I asked her to investigate the staff, and she does not believe it is magically protected as such. As it is so powerful in itself, I believe Silas is quite arrogant about his ability to defend himself. Molsa thinks he may be waiting until the staff is fully restored before adding a specific protective charm or substance.'

Willow brightened. 'So you think my plan could work?'

'It's a good plan,' agreed Moreg. 'Simple but far from easy. As I see it, there's only one problem.'

'How to actually find the Craegun?' guessed Willow. 'Well, I've thought about that too.'

'Why am I not surprised?' said Moreg, lips twitching.

Willow nodded. 'I think, if anyone might have an idea, it would probably be Feathering. He's been alive for centuries.' She hoped the cloud dragon might know of a way to find the mythical beast.

'I fink **SO** too,' said Oswin. '**Besides,** even if 'e doesn't know **anyfings**, we'd need 'im if we goes ter the **montins** cos flyin' sticks **won't** work. They freezes.'

Moreg nodded. 'He's right. The air at the top of the mountains is sub-zero. A broomstick would likely freeze while we were flying, which could be incredibly dangerous.'

'Oh dear,' said Essential, pushing her glasses up.

Willow nodded. 'Then we have to find him and ask for his help. I'll see if Sometimes can send a message to him through pepper-tea communication.'

Willow dozed off on the chair beside the window, with its view of the Great Wisperia Tree below surrounded by clouds, while they waited for Feathering to arrive.

She wasn't the only one. Essential and Oswin were fast asleep on the kitchen chairs, Sometimes on the sofa, and Beroc finally slept too, soothed by the hedge

witch's remedies. Only Moreg and Pimpernell stayed alert, sending steam-kettle messages to Rubix and other Enchancil members about Silas and his plans to create a new iron half-moon. To be completely safe, they didn't tell anyone about their own plans, just in case the messages ended up in the wrong hands.

Willow was just waking up when Moreg received one from Twist's aunts, the Howling sisters. In steamy words above their heads, there was a call to battle.

The elves have declared war on the Brothers of Wol. We go to fight now.

Soon other messages appeared, with similar declarations from other Enchancil members, speaking on behalf of their various tribes and countries. Dwarfs, trolls, Mementons and humans.

Moreg and the others stared at the words above their heads, their faces solemn.

A war was beginning.

17

The Journey Begins

It was afternoon when Feathering arrived, landing on a nearby branch as big as a road with a *whoosh* that shook the windows. Willow, Oswin and Essential tore out of the treehouse to greet him, followed closely by Moreg.

'Willow!' cried Feathering. 'Moreg, Essential. I got your message that you needed me. On my flight here, I saw many creatures marching. They appear to be heading towards the fortress of Wolkana. Thundera followed them to see what was happening, but I came straight here.'

Moreg nodded, filling him in on everything that had happened – how Twist had been captured in order for Silas to repair the elf staff, and how the elves had declared war on the Brothers of Wol, with many other of Starfell's tribes, creatures and people doing the same.

He looked stricken. 'Another war. I'd hoped it wouldn't come to that!'

Willow nodded. 'Us too, Feathering. But we might be able to stop the worst of it by getting the elf staff back from Silas,' and she explained their plan to find the Craegun so that she could get her magic back.

Feathering reared up on his hind legs. The tree branch swayed, brown leaves raining down upon their heads. 'You think finding the Craegun is the solution? Willow, I'm sorry, but you're wrong! The stories I have heard of this monster are the stuff of nightmares. The Craegun is not some kindly beast who will want to help. The mountains are treacherous, and to reach him there are obstacles and tricks, each one designed to test you, torment you, dissuade you . . . and even if you pass them all, and very, very few have, there's a price – and it's always higher than most are prepared to pay!'

Willow swallowed. 'I know. I didn't mean to make it sound like I thought it would be easy. It won't be – I know that. But what other choice do we have? There's no way into the fortress. If we do nothing, Silas will use Twist's blood in four days' time, repair the elf staff, and then our world could *die*. Look at the Great Wisperia Tree.' Tears flooded her eyes.

Moreg nodded. 'It's starting to happen already.'

Feathering, Essential and Oswin all turned as if they were looking at it for the first time.

'What's happened to it?' breathed Essential.

'It's dying. It needs us,' said Willow. 'Whatever Silas has been doing, the way he's been abusing magic, it's destroying Starfell.' She took a deep breath. 'The world is beginning to sicken because of *me*. If it wasn't for me bringing back the vanished kingdom, the elf staff would be safe, buried beneath the ground. We'd *all* be safe. That's why I have to do something.'

'**Well, 'tis MY fault an' all!**' cried Oswin, who looked on the verge of blowing up, his patchy fur turning a faded orange. '**I made that mer-king oo was afraid o' cats fink I wos one, so he woulds release the staffs ter yew. That's when the Silas cumberworld came along an' stole it, an' yer magic too.**'

Willow felt her heart melt. Had he been feeling guilty all this time? She bent down and touched his ragged fur. Was that one of the main causes for his hair loss?

'I feel exactly the same,' said Moreg. 'I should have realised earlier that my visions were being obscured.'

'Me too,' said Feathering. 'I was there. I even

encouraged you. I never once stopped to think that we were being tricked – and I'm a lot older. I should have known better.'

'Oh, Feathering, how could you have?'

'Well, how could you?' he countered.

Willow felt something hard and painful finally seem to soften inside her belly. It was the guilt she'd been carrying all this time.

Granny Flossy's voice floated inside her mind. *'It's okay ter feel bad when you've done something wrong, child, but you can't change the past, you can only learn from it – that's how you make peace with it. Tough emotions like guilt and shame shrink when we shine a light on them and talk about them. They grow when we keep them in the dark. Don't make a home for them, or they'll never leave.'*

Willow realised that they'd *all* felt responsible, and maybe that wasn't necessarily a bad thing. It was

good to learn from what had happened, but it was also good to share their regret, to remember it wasn't just Willow who had been fooled.

'We were *all* tricked by Silas. But I can't let that define who I am and make me never want to help again. That way he wins once more. By going to the mountains and finding the Craegun, there is a chance to put things right, to get the elf staff, save Twist and stop a war. I've got to at least try.'

Feathering stared at her as if he were making up his mind. 'You're right.'

Essential nodded, then pushed up her glasses. 'Mad as it seems, this might be the only way.'

Moreg had been looking contemplative. 'I do like to think things through carefully, but Willow is right. Having weighed up all the options, I too can see no way forward but this. Could I take the half-moon to Wolkana on Willow's behalf and attempt to bring Silas out? Perhaps. But the elf staff is the most powerful tool in Starfell's history, even without its ability to take magic away, and, so long as Silas has it at his disposal, I would have no hope of defeating him. The clearest way to stop him is to remove the staff from him altogether, instantly. That means Willow

must steal it back, using her ability to make things disappear, and it seems there is only one option left to restore her magic. Plus, according to what Sometimes has perceived, even the magic of Starfell itself is encouraging Willow on this path.'

The witch met her eyes. 'You won't face the Craegun alone, Willow. I will help.'

'**Me an' all,**' said Oswin.

'And me,' said Essential.

'Of course,' said Feathering.

'Thank you, everyone,' said Willow, touched.

There was the sound of footsteps from behind, and they saw Sometimes and Pimpernell coming outside to join them.

The hedge witch looked solemn. 'I think it'll be best if I take Beroc back ter me tower, where I can better care for 'im. 'Sides, me other patients be needin' me.'

Willow and the others nodded, and they helped to carry Beroc outside to the Ambulbroom. Pimpernell clicked a lever to collapse one of the tall upright chairs into a stretcher, and Willow and Essential strapped him in securely.

Then they all said their farewells and watched as Pimpernell left, the Ambulbroom flying against the

late-afternoon sky, which was beginning to turn from apricot to gold.

Sometimes touched Willow's shoulder, making her jump.

'Sorry,' he said, running a hand bashfully through his white hair. His large blue eyes looked sad but earnest. 'So you've got them to agree to go to the mountains of Nach?' he asked.

Willow wondered if he'd guessed or read her memories. It didn't matter. She nodded, and he smiled.

'I want to come too, truly, but I feel that there is something I must try here first, for the Great Wisperia Tree. I don't think I should leave it.'

Willow nodded, then squeezed his arm. 'I understand, Sometimes. I think you should stay too. It's important. I hope there's something that can help.'

'Thanks.'

Moreg patted her cloak, then she began to pull out large, hairy coats from her portal pantry. 'I knew there was a reason I'd felt the urge to stock my pantry with these in the autumn. I mean, there's usually a reason . . . eventually.'

Willow couldn't help but smile. 'Practical makes perfect.'

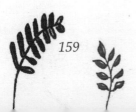

The witch grinned in return, then shrugged into a grey coat and handed over the other two. Willow put on a huge, soft white one while Essential chose the big, shaggy black one.

'We're really going to the mountains of Nach,' Willow murmured. For a small moment, she wished she could tell Granny Flossy.

Then they said goodbye to Sometimes and climbed aboard the cloud dragon, who launched himself up into the sky.

In Willow's pocket, the StoryPass switched to '*Turning Point*'.

18

The Mountains of Nach

They flew over the canopy of the forest of Wisperia, only it wasn't the beautiful sight that always stopped Willow's heart. From above, at a dragon's pace, Willow finally saw how bad things had really got. Half of the forest, usually a colourful burst of blues and pinks, green and bright orange, had begun to fade to a dull grey.

'**Oh** no,' whispered Oswin.

'It's much worse than I feared,' said Willow.

As night fell, the air grew cool, and the sky was studded with stars.

'It'll be hours still,' called Feathering. 'I suggest you get some sleep on the flight over.'

Willow wasn't the only one grateful for the opportunity to rest. She, Essential and Oswin had

taken a short nap earlier, but they were all feeling the effects of staying up all night. Moreg handed round some rope from her portal pantry, and they strapped themselves to the dragon so they could rest safely.

They all fell into a deep slumber as Feathering flew over forest and glades, lakes and vast shimmering seas, through rain and sweltering heat as they passed the desert of Troll Country.

They finally awoke early the next morning, when dawn was cresting the sky.

Oswin rummaged in the hairy carpetbag and handed round a jar of biscuits for breakfast. But Willow wasn't hungry. She still felt exhausted, despite having slept.

She inched forward towards Feathering's ears. 'Are you okay? You've been flying for hours. Do you need a break?'

'I wouldn't mind actually,' he admitted.

He came down to land near a river, and they all climbed off so that Feathering could get some water and rest. Oswin went to help him fish out some of the larger bugs that had got stuck to his teeth on the flight.

'Ugh,' said Essential with a repulsed shiver as she watched Oswin eat one.

'**Wot?**' he said.

'Willow,' said Essential, looking at her, 'it's time for your tonic, I think. You're looking a bit pale. After Moreg arrived and we got word that we needed to go to Wisperia, I made sure I packed some just in case.'

Willow stared at her in awe. She hadn't even seen her scurry off to fetch the tonic before they'd left.

'You're brilliant, thank you – I must admit, I'm feeling exhausted.'

Willow took the proffered bottle gratefully and drank the tonic. After a while, most of the exhaustion fell away, and she felt almost normal again. 'Thank you.'

Essential shrugged like it was nothing, but it wasn't. Not to Willow.

Soon afterwards, Feathering was ready to continue. 'It's not far from here now. You might want some more layers.'

They were all wearing heavy furs already.

'**Oh, me greedy aunt,**' whispered Oswin.

Even Moreg looked stricken. 'This is all we have.'

Feathering sighed. 'Well, nothing we can do about that now.'

They climbed aboard, and Feathering launched himself once more into the sky. The air grew steadily

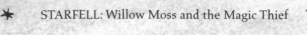

colder, the landscape turning ever more wild and vast, blanketed by snow. They were entering the mountains of Nach at last.

There was a familiar loud wailing from Oswin. **'Oh no, oh, me 'orrid aunt!'**

Willow frowned. 'What is it?' she asked.

But, all too soon, they discovered just what it was for themselves. A blizzard.

Out of nowhere, snow was now falling fast and in all directions. And it was bone-chillingly freezing.

The sound of large teeth chattering loudly told them that even Feathering was feeling it. The dragon was slowing down. It was hard even to see your hand in front of your face.

Willow swallowed. 'Oswin, the storm light.'

The kobold rummaged inside the carpetbag, then handed her the tiny light. Willow held it aloft, and it began to glow.

Suddenly they could see beyond the white onslaught, and they all screamed. They were heading right into the side of a mountain.

Feathering whirled upwards, but not quickly enough – they crashed on to a rocky ledge covered in snow.

Willow, Essential and Moreg went flying. Essential held up her hands to slow them down with her magic, but they were still falling fast. And, even as they whirled towards the edge of the mountain, there was still space, incredibly, in Willow's mind to think: *COLD.*

It was utterly, unbelievably freezing cold. The sort of cold that cut like a knife.

Moreg managed to clasp Essential's hand to lend her power, lightning crackled round them, and they

slowed completely. They landed in a mound of heavy snow, hard enough to scrape knees, shins and cheeks on the rocks beneath – but thankfully not hard enough to break any bones – and they came to a juddering stop a whisper from the mountain edge.

'Oh, my friends, I'm so sorry!' cried Feathering, flying down to join them.

'That's o-okay,' mumbled Willow, her face planted in the snow. The tiny lantern was still clutched in her frozen hand when she sat up.

To her horror, she saw the carpetbag was leaning precariously over the precipice, so she crawled to it and managed to snatch it back.

From within the bag, she could hear, '**Oh no, oh no, oh** *nooooooo.*'

'It's okay,' said Willow, her heart in her throat. 'You're safe now.'

'**I doubts that very much.**'

'Why?' asked Willow.

A paw crept out of the bag. It was covered in icicles and pointing, shakily, to something that was heading their way. '**G-G-GIANT!**'

As one, Willow, Essential, Moreg and Feathering turned to look in the direction Oswin was indicating,

167

squinting their eyes against the swirling blizzard.

They looked up.

Then up some more.

And blinked.

It was, indeed, a giant.

19

The Giant's Hut

A seventeen-foot giant was leering down at them. It was like a small mountain itself.

There was a sound like the wind howling through a corridor in an old house, which Willow realised was the giant sighing. Then the next thing she knew it was picking them up as if they were the size of birds.

'**Oh, me greedy aunt Osbertrude! A pox on yew from all the kobolds!**' hissed Oswin.

'A fiery dragon pox from me as well,' added Feathering.

'*Aghhhhhhh!*' screamed Willow and Essential, who didn't have space beyond their fear for insults.

'You may regret this,' warned Moreg.

The giant ignored them all as they squirmed,

169

placing them inside a pouch slung across its torso. It was dark inside, and soft, and smelt of something wild and leathery.

Willow's heart hammered in her chest. How could they have survived almost falling from a mountain ledge just to be kidnapped by a giant? Was their journey to find the Craegun over before it had begun?

They all struggled to stand, crashing back and forth and falling head over feet as the giant took slow, lumbering steps up the mountain.

'This is, frankly, *undignified*,' muttered Feathering.

Suddenly the wild rocking stopped, and Willow and her friends all collapsed in a heap on Feathering's belly.

They heard the creak of a huge door, and then a slam as it shuddered in its hinges. The whistling noise of the blizzard had died down somewhat.

Willow scrambled to the flap of the pouch and lifted it up to see what was happening . . .

. . . Only to jump back in fright as she saw a pair of enormous eyes blinking down at them.

'Oh, me greedy **aunt**, is this 'OW we ends?!' howled Oswin.

170

As the giant flipped the pouch open and its massive fingers reached inside again, Willow and Essential screamed and tried to run away, like ants in a jar. Moreg, however, was blasting it with lightning.

The giant shook its stony fingers as if they'd been stung – then came back for them. It plucked them out – surprisingly gently, Willow noticed – and placed them on an enormous slab of wood.

Scrambling to her feet in panic, Willow realised they were on a giant's table . . . and she *really* hoped they weren't lunch.

The giant sighed as they blinked up at it.

'Well, that was pretty stupid,' it said in a perfectly ordinary voice. She was a female, Willow realised. 'What on Great Starfell made you come to the mountains of Nach in a blizzard?'

'Skadi?' said Moreg in surprise.

'Moreg?' The stony giant blinked down at her. 'Well, I never.'

Willow and Essential whirled round to look at Moreg. Even Feathering seemed surprised.

'You know her?' asked Willow, feeling relief flood her senses. Perhaps they weren't going to end up as a giant's meal after all.

'Yes. Though I must say I never expected to be carried around in her *purse.*' Then the witch gave what almost looked like a smile. 'I might leave that part of the story out.'

The giant grinned, revealing teeth like boulders. 'Yep, I would. Though I suppose you could add it to your repertoire of rumours – tea parties with the dead, trapping spirits in snow globes . . .'

'Snow globes? That's a new one.'

'Not around these parts,' said the giant.

And then Willow startled as the giant began to shrink.

'What on Starfell?' exclaimed Essential.

Before they knew it, they were staring down from the table at a woman dressed head to toe in fur coverings, who was still rather tall for a human, but certainly no longer giant. She began to take off her furs and hang them up on a series of pegs on the wall, which Willow noticed had been fitted at human height. In fact, now she took a moment to look round the enormous hut, she realised that apart from the enormous table the rest of the furniture was more human-sized.

'B-b-but?' said Willow. 'You were a giant?'

The woman raised a brow as she began to remove a heavy snowshoe. She looked a bit affronted.

'I beg your pardon – I am *still* a giant.'

'Um,' said Willow.

'I am a shrink giant obviously. My name's Skadi.'

From the hairy carpetbag, there was a faint, **'Oh,'** of realisation from Oswin, but he was clearly the only one who had heard of them.

'I'll get us down,' suggested Feathering, and they all climbed on to his back, and the cloud dragon flew them the short distance to the floor.

'You're a giant that can shrink?' asked Essential as they approached Skadi. She pushed up her glasses, then frowned as she noticed one of her lenses had cracked during their fall in the snow.

Skadi nodded. 'Yes, that's the idea. It is believed that somewhere in our ancestry – we're talking thousands of years here – as more and more people started creeping within our borders, and the giants didn't have as much space to roam, some of us started to shrink accordingly. Not the great ice giants, or some of the long giants obviously, but the rest of us, yes,' she said with a small sigh.

As Willow looked round the hut again, a thought struck her. She reached inside the hairy carpetbag, took out her granny's notebook and paged through

until she found a sketch she'd seen the day before. She peered at it, then back at the hut.

'It's the same one!' she cried.

'The same what?' said Feathering.

'Look!' she cried, showing the others. 'This hut! A long time ago, Granny Flossy lived here.'

They all looked at the sketch. Changes had occurred over time, like the addition of the enormous table, and at one point there used to be a large cauldron by the fireplace. 'And above here,' said Willow, touching the mantelpiece that had the same knot in the wood as the one in the drawing, 'she would dry her herbs.'

Skadi turned to Willow. 'You're Flossy Mossy's granddaughter?'

Willow nodded.

'Wow,' said Skadi. 'She gave me this hut after her accident, when your parents came to fetch her. They had a hard time persuading her to stay with them, but I believe you were the one who convinced her. She sent me a letter not long afterwards to tell me all about what happened on the day she came to live with you.'

Willow blinked. Suddenly the memory washed over her.

*

It was raining, and Granny was being led into the cottage against her will by a young Camille, who was using her magical ability to move Granny Flossy with her mind.

'Look, child,' Granny had snapped, turning to glare at the young girl, 'I'd have a rethink sharpish about whether you want ter keep trying this. I might have done this ter myself by accident –' she pointed at her wild green hair – 'but I can promise yer, I know how ter do it on purpose.' Granny's boots continued to slide for half a step, so she added, 'Think hard, child. This ain't dye . . . Ye'll be like that fer life.'

Camille raised a hand to her raven tresses, which she was rather vain about, and hesitated.

Her mother, however, snapped, 'Don't listen to her. Keep pushing, Camille.'

It was Willow, standing just behind them in the shadows, who raced to intervene.

'Come on, Granny,' she'd said. 'Your room is ready upstairs, and I picked those flowers you like.'

177

'Oh, for Wol's sake, Willow Moss!' cried her mother. 'Don't tell me you've brought a bunch of stinkweed into the house!'

Willow had blinked. 'Um . . . I filled all the vases I could find. Why?'

'Great Starfell,' her father breathed, his eyes wide.

'Oh, Willow, you're as bad as Granny Flossy! You know that they explode, don't you? Letting off the most awful scent?'

Willow had not. 'Oh, so that's why it's called stinkweed.'

The others had closed their eyes and groaned, but Granny had cackled with delight. She'd then come forward to take Willow's hand, allowing herself to be led inside the cottage at last.

Later, while Willow's mother cleared out all the stinkweed and used seven cleaning potions to tackle the smell, Willow watched Granny Flossy unpack her hairy green carpetbag in her attic room. Everything inside the bag was a shade of green – her dresses, her coats, her underwear, and even her socks.

'You must really like green,' Willow had observed.

Granny frowned. 'Must I?'

Willow blinked. 'Well, all your things . . .'

'So because my things are green you assume I must like the colour?'

Willow was confused. 'Don't you?'

'Don't I what?'

'Like the colour green?'

Granny thought about that as she folded a particularly lumpy green dress. 'I don't mind it, I suppose, but it's not my favourite colour.'

'But then why are all your things green?' said Willow in surprise.

Granny gave her a small, satisfied smile. Then she tapped the side of her nose. 'See now that is the better question. You looked and made an assumption – my things are green, therefore I must really like the colour. But that is not observing, that is drawing a conclusion without considering all the evidence.'

Willow then looked at everything, including Granny's hair, and said, 'Was it from the accident? Did all your things turn green, like your hair?'

'Now that is a good theory. And you are correct.' Granny looked impressed.

There was a soft hoot outside from a passing owl. It was late, and Willow should have been in bed already, but Granny didn't seem to worry about

179

things like that. She pulled out a notebook from her hairy green carpetbag.

'What's that?' Willow asked.

'Just my notebook. Every potion-maker keeps one for their experiments. I use it to record me own observations, child, about potions and ingredients . . . life too. It all goes inter the mix somehow. Whenever I find something interesting, I make a point of writing it down.'

'Oh,' said Willow, reaching to touch the pages. Then she looked round the attic, trying to see what could possibly have been interesting enough to note down. It was full of old furniture and dust.

'I'm writing about unexpected allies and silver linings,' said Granny. 'In short, about my remarkable grandchild.'

'Oh,' said Willow, thinking of Camille using her magic.

Perhaps Granny could read her mind because she said, 'I meant you, Willow.'

'Me?'

'Oh yes. When everyone else tried force, you tried something else.'

'What was that?' asked Willow.

180

'Love. Kindness. It's amazing how much people underestimate their power.'

'Oh,' Willow said again. She wasn't sure that she'd done anything that special really. She did know, though, that it was the first time anyone had ever called her remarkable. The feeling inside was new and delicate, and it made her toes curl, like she wanted to squirm but also draw closer to it all at once.

Then she looked at her grandmother as something else occurred to her.

'What is your favourite colour?' asked Willow.

Granny grinned. 'Right now, I'd have to say it's the shade your mother turned when she realised the house had been doused with stinkweed.'

Willow smiled at the memory. It was incredible to think that this hut had once belonged to Granny Flossy – that she'd invented some of her best potions here.

'Is that why you're here?' asked Skadi. 'Because of Flossy?'

'Yes and no,' said Willow. 'In a way, Granny has

helped to guide us here. We need to find someone . . .
Well, a beast . . .'

'A beast?' echoed Skadi.

'The Craegun,' said Moreg, her face solemn.

'You can't be serious, Moreg . . . Even *you* wouldn't
dare to look for the *Craegun*.'

'We have no choice,' said Feathering.

Skadi looked at him. 'What do you mean?'

And they explained – about the world, the damage
it was suffering, what Silas was planning. The danger
Twist was in. The war.

Skadi sighed. 'So then I wasn't imagining it.'

'Imagining what?' asked Willow.

The shrink giant looked grave. 'It's better if I
show you.'

20

The Giant's Garden

They followed Skadi as she led them to a wooden door at the side of the hut.

'Flossy Mossy started this years ago, but I must say that I probably went a bit overboard.'

She opened the back door, which was half the size of the enormous front door, but still twice the size of a normal one, and Willow and her friends stepped into what felt like another world.

'When I'm in my full form, I have to duck to use this door, but it's manageable,' said Skadi. 'I wanted to ensure I could use it in all my forms.'

It was an enormous terrarium, filled with plants so big they towered over Willow, Moreg and Essential. Even Feathering looked small by comparison. So much of it was green and lush and full of incredible

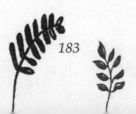

flowers – some the size of their heads. Willow thought for a moment that she knew what a fairy might feel like.

'Flossy Mossy started it as a kind of small kitchen

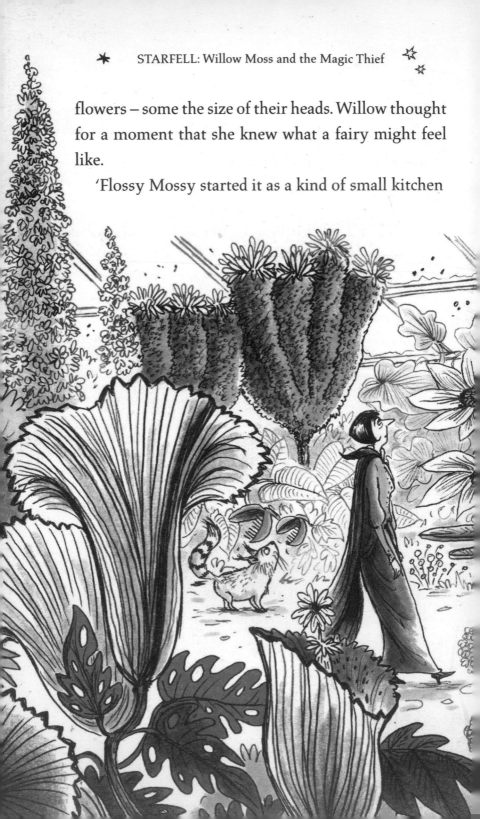

garden to grow some useful plants – as well as a few more extraordinary ones for her potion experiments,' Skadi said, pointing at a bunch of enormous purple plants.

'But I made it bigger, and installed special glass from the famed glass-blowers in Hutia,' she said, pointing upwards, 'so that I wasn't just limited to specimens that grew on the mountains. But using this –' she came to a box – 'I could still grow some of my favourites.'

'Never-melt ice?' Willow guessed.

'Yes! But last week I started noticing these . . . spots.'

Willow felt her heart sink as the shrink giant showed them some of the plants, which were covered in familiar black spots, like on the trees in Wisperia and elsewhere.

'Also a lot of my trees have started changing.'

Skadi led them to a section near the back, where the trees had turned a strange, dull grey.

'I couldn't understand it. I mean, this is such a controlled environment. Many of these plants wouldn't survive outside, so I thought that somehow I had done this to them, introduced something odd.'

Willow shook her head. 'It's happening everywhere,' she said.

'And you really believe it's magic – that it's suffering?'

Willow nodded.

Skadi looked at her plants sadly. She reminded Willow so much of Nolin Sometimes in that moment. She knew just how much the two would probably have liked each other, and how much Sometimes was hurting over the damage to his beloved forest.

'We're going to try and fix it. That's why we need to find the Craegun.'

Skadi drew a long breath. She looked at Willow, then at Moreg. 'All right. But you will need far more than my help. The Craegun is almost impossible to find, not without a guide. There is a boy who might be able to assist you.'

'A boy?' asked Essential.

'Yes,' confirmed Skadi, touching a tree that was covered in icicles. 'The legend goes that when he was very small he got stuck on the second mountain with his mother. The mountains from there on are all Craegun country, you see. They got lost during Eir, the snow month. The boy died, but then his mother made a bargain with the beast: her magic in exchange for her child's life. The Craegun agreed, and he turned the boy into one of frost.'

Willow's mouth fell open. 'I've heard that story! Granny Flossy wrote it down in here,' she said,

187

holding up the notebook.

Essential looked thoughtful. 'If the Craegun restores lost things, why didn't the boy turn into an ordinary human again? Why is he made of frost?' she asked.

'A good question,' said Feathering. 'I believe it would be because the Craegun works with magic in bargains and exchanges.'

'That's right,' said Skadi. 'His mother gave up her magic so that the Craegun could use it to bring the child back. The boy kept his identity, but his original life was not restored as such; he was offered a new lease of life in a magical form.'

'It would have benefited him too,' Moreg noted. 'Being made of ice and frost, he would be well equipped to survive the journey home with his mother.'

Skadi nodded. 'The boy is renowned here in the mountains. Ever since the Craegun revived him, they seem to have a connection. He can sense the beast and the mountains themselves. He will know how to find the Craegun. We can leave first thing in the morning.'

Willow hesitated. 'Can't we go now? It's just, we only have three days to stop Silas.'

Skadi shook her head. 'That blizzard I found you in? It's only going to get stronger. They call it a Giant's

surprise because even in giant form we wouldn't be able to pass through it, and we will need our wits about us as the boy lives on the second mountain.'

Moreg nodded. 'Less haste, more speed. We can use this time to rest and to prepare.'

That night they ate a rich stew full of green mountain potatoes, peas and herm fruit. It was delicious.

Skadi showed them all how to tie different knots in rope, how to sling it round themselves and throw it over cliffs, how to use ice picks. She handed out extra trousers, earmuffs and gloves, and they stocked Moreg's portal pantry with loads of dried meat and fruit, and canisters of melted snow.

Moreg had several purple sleeping bags in her pantry, also kept for some unknown event, and they all curled up before the fire, snuggling into them.

Oswin was the first to go to sleep at Willow's feet, but soon the hut was filled with the sound of gentle snoring.

Willow fell asleep quickly, but woke up sometime after midnight. She couldn't help looking around at the slumbering forms and wishing that they were moving. There was so much to do, and they didn't

have time to waste. Her heart started to race when she thought of poor Twist, frightened and alone, with Silas.

She went to get a glass of water, then fetched Granny Flossy's notebook and opened it by the dying embers of the fire. Outside the wind howled, and the night sky was grey and full of white, swirling snow, but by the fire it was cosy and comfortable.

She found an entry that made her pause because, even now, it felt like Granny was there, giving Willow advice, telling her exactly what she needed to hear.

It's summer in the mountains, which to the casual observer doesn't look that different to winter, but there are differences: more flowers in bloom, more sunshine and fewer snowstorms. It is one of the best times to go sample picking, traversing the mountain and finding unusual plants that grow only in this season - which lasts just a few short weeks.

A couple of days ago, I was struck down with a cold, which I realised would delay my

sample picking, so I brewed up a simple potion that would stop it in its tracks. I felt better, so I went out.

After a day or two, though, the cold returned, so I came back and did the same thing again, making myself a stronger potion that would delay the onset of the cold. Well, it did. But the weather turned, and an unseasonal snowstorm arrived, lasting a week.

When the storm was over, my cold was back and so was the good weather. I made another potion to delay the cold further. But this time my body said no. It didn't work. So instead I took to my bed.

The cold passed in three days with rest and some of Skadi's bearfrost soup. Three days. Afterwards, summer was over. I had put off dealing with something that would only last three days, and instead ensured that I felt worse for longer . . . There's a lesson in this somewhere. I suppose it's that if we give more to ourselves in times of need, we can get more from ourselves later.

Willow touched the final words of the entry. Bodies, including her own, needed sleep and rest, and, if they fought that, their bodies would fight back. They would be stronger in the long run if they allowed themselves to pause.

It was something special to read Granny's words in the place where she'd written them. It was like she was there with her, and it comforted Willow. She put the book down, closed her eyes, and tried to take Granny Flossy's good advice.

In the morning, at first light, Skadi reported that the storm had died down.

They had a simple breakfast of dried apples, and mountain bread that was black and as hard as rock. Skadi also offered them a cheese that she said was made from the milk of Nach mountain goats, which Willow and Essential declined. It was bright green, like the animals' milk and fur apparently.

Willow and Essential had shared a look over the cheese – one that said, *'Perhaps not.'*

But Oswin asked for thirds.

Moreg managed to roll out an entire barrel of apples for Feathering from her portal pantry, and

another one that was full of cloudleaf, a kind of purple-and-pink foliage that grew just outside the Cloud Mountains.

'Something told me to pick this a few months ago,' she said.

'Fantastic,' said Feathering, who began eating the lot. 'Also, quite wise,' he added seriously, 'having a light repast, so we're not overly sluggish when we set off. Nothing worse than flying with a bloated belly.'

'That's a *light repast*?' said Oswin. 'Wot do ych 'ave when it's a big'un? A herd o' cattle?'

Feathering shrugged. 'Sometimes. Though I'm really trying to be more of a vegetarian these days.'

'Oh.'

Willow watched this exchange with a mixture of amusement and anxiety. She really wanted to get going, painfully aware of how vital it was that they find the Craegun. Right then, it felt almost impossible.

Moreg looked at her. 'Willow, if anyone can do this, it's you.' She gave a small laugh. 'You remind me so much of myself when I was your age.'

Willow's mouth fell open. 'I remind you of *you*?'

'Say wot now?' breathed Oswin, eyes wide.

193

'Willow, you might not realise this, but you have a quiet strength that is remarkable. I don't think many people are quite as determined as you.'

'Oh **well**, that's **true 'nuf**,' said Oswin. 'I **fought yew wos gonna** say **sumfink else**, cos she doesn't mek **me** knees turn ter **water** when she lewks at me.'

Moreg looked at him with her eyes like razors.

Oswin turned a pallid shade of green in fright. '*Exacterly.*'

Moreg's lips twitched. Then her eyes turned white, which really set Oswin off.

'Oh **noooo**! Oh, me '**orrid** aunt Osbertrude! Oh, a **curse** is upon me . . .'

'I see a . . . boy.'

'Oh **right**,' said Oswin, clearing his throat. '**Yew wos** 'aving a *visions*. I **k n e w** that.'

There was a low, tinkly sound that was Feathering laughing.

Moreg continued, ignoring Oswin's outburst. 'It's the child made of frost. He senses that we are here.'

Skadi blinked and set down a huge mug of tea with a thud. 'He does?'

'He's waiting for us at the bottom of the first mountain.'

21

The Boy Made of Frost

There was a heavy silence.

'He's waiting for us?' said Willow.

Moreg nodded. 'Perhaps Magic has also shown him that he needs to help you, like it tried to tell you that you needed to come here.'

Skadi nodded. 'It's possible. He senses the mountains, which, like all things, are entwined with magic. It doesn't surprise me that he knows you're here.'

Then the shrink giant stood up, put on her outer layers of clothing and began to grow, enlarging once more into a huge figure.

She opened the door. There was still a heavy snowfall and a strong wind howling outside.

'It hasn't quite died down as much as I'd have liked,' she said. 'It is clear enough for me, but I'm not

sure about humans, or indeed dragons. I think it's best if I carry you in my bag again.'

'Thank you, but I would prefer to fly,' said Feathering with dignity, making his way outside . . . where his feathers and scales instantly turned to ice.

He reversed back indoors quickly, his limbs stiff and his wings momentarily frozen in place. 'On second thoughts . . .'

The shrink giant looked at him with her stony gaze. 'Not like I've lived here my whole life and know what I'm talking about, dragon.'

Feathering gave her a wry grin. 'Apologies.'

The giant smiled in return. 'Yeah, I would have done the same thing, to be fair.'

Then she held out her bag and, somewhat reluctantly, they all climbed inside. It began to sway as Skadi picked them up, and once again Willow and Essential started doing somersaults. Before Willow lost her footing again, she had time to glance at Moreg, who was standing in a strange way with her legs firmly planted.

'Lead shoes,' explained Moreg. 'Doesn't help when someone tries witch-drowning, though – well, apart from when you give them a good kick . . .'

196

But soon the swaying evened out as Skadi, hearing their screams, cupped the purse between her giant palms and trudged through the snow slowly and laboriously.

There was a low moan from Oswin in the hairy carpetbag. 'I **fink** I might be sick . . .'

Willow felt sick and dizzy too, and the cold still filtered into the giant's bag through gaps in the fabric, making them all shiver.

Finally, they came to a halt. Skadi put the bag on the ground, and Willow and her friends climbed out.

The blizzard had finally stopped, and they were able to see the mountains of Nach clearly for the first time.

From their vantage point at the bottom of the first mountain they could see the rest of the vast expanse of peaks rising into the distance like a splayed white hand. They were surrounded by tall, spindly trees, their limbs laden with snow. The sky above them waltzed in shades of green and purple. It was breathtaking.

From the valley in front of them, they could make out a hazy figure coming towards them, becoming clearer the closer it got. They saw a snowy owl beat

its wings against the sky, hooting softly as it landed on the outstretched arm of a boy made of frost. He was tall and thin, with jagged ice for hair. He walked towards them and then paused before the giant, turning blind eyes towards them.

The shrink giant telescoped down. The boy held out his hand and took Skadi's in his own, writing something inside her palm.

'What's he doing?' asked Essential.

'I think it's his way of communicating,' Willow said, remembering what Granny Flossy had written in her notebook. 'He's deaf and blind, but he can write in people's palms.'

'That's right,' said Skadi. 'Sometimes he spells out words, but when he wants to show you what he can sense from the world around him, like how the mountain feels and sometimes what it dreams, he draws pictures into the palms of his companions instead, and they come to life.'

That was happening now, Willow realised. They all gasped in wonder as one of these images began to grow from the shrink giant's outstretched hand, made of snowflakes, wind and enchantment.

They saw a cave and, inside it, a pair of pinpricks for eyes, burning in the darkness.

Willow swallowed.

'The Craegun!' cried Feathering.

Skadi nodded. Willow stepped forward to introduce herself to the boy.

199

He sensed her presence and held out his hand. As soon as she touched it, he smiled, then turned her hand over and drew something on her palm that rose up into an image that shimmered in the air.

It was a girl. She was short with straight hair and eyes that turned up at the corners. She looked tired and frightened. In her arms was a carpetbag. Something blinked at them from a hole in the bag, then disappeared.

Willow gasped. 'That's me!'

She took his palm and spelt out with her finger what she'd said aloud.

The boy nodded, seeming pleased at how quickly she had grasped how to communicate with him, and he wrote a message in return: Magic wanted you to come. But it won't be easy. The Craegun would never allow it to be.

Willow read his message aloud, then swallowed and wrote back: **So you will help us to find him?**

He nodded again, then he wrote something else in her palm.

'Lumi,' she read aloud, and the frosty word melted as soon as it had appeared.

Is that your name?

Yes, he replied.

Willow took his palm and spelt out her own name: **Willow. That's mine.**

The boy smiled in return. Then into her palm he drew shapes. These grew until they could all see a vast frozen river, followed by a massive mountain range. The wind howled, and something tiny struggled against the blizzard. Lumi waved the frosty image away and then wrote: It will be dangerous. You could die.

Willow repeated what he'd said to the others, then

replied: **I have to. It's not for me, it's for Starfell. If I don't ask the Craegun for my magic back, our world could die.**

The boy nodded. I have sensed a change too. It is growing sick. This is why I will help you. But I must warn you, the way is treacherous. Very few people ever make it through the second mountain, which acts as a barrier to the third mountain – if we succeed, at a certain point your companions will have to leave you.

Willow's heart clenched, and her gaze darted to her friends. But Lumi continued.

Because from there, you will begin the test of the Craegun. I will guide you, but I will not be able to help you. There will be three trials. Each one will challenge a different side of you. They are unique, shaped with you in mind. That is why they are so hard. But I believe you will endure.

Willow swallowed. **I understand. Thank you,** she wrote back. Then she told the others what Lumi had said.

'So yew **means** before **Willow** even gets **ter** the Craegun we coulds **all** die on the second montin?' asked Oswin, his eyes wide and scared.

Skadi nodded. 'There's a lot of ground to cover, and much danger to encounter. A wild magic acts as a kind

of protective guardian of the Craegun's land.'

Willow turned to her companions. 'You . . . You can all turn back,' she said.

But her friends wouldn't hear of it.

'We're here with you, Willow, for as long as we can be,' said Moreg.

Essential squeezed her hand.

Lumi indicated that they should follow him, to enter the dangerous territory of the second mountain.

Willow took a deep breath. 'Here we go,' she said.

'Oh, me aunt,' said Essential, which caused a few of the others to laugh despite their nerves.

As they moved on through the remote landscape, the dazzling swirling lights of the sky ahead seemed to enhance how vast and beautiful the snowy mountains were, but also how treacherous. Now, with the clear sky, Willow could see how dangerous it would be to be stuck out here alone.

They walked for miles through thick, knee-high snow.

Lumi had been right that they had to keep their wits about them. Along the way, they encountered strange sprites that seemed to sing to them, offering to help –

203

but Skadi warned them they were tricksters who led people astray . . . in good time too as Essential was following one, her eyes behind her cracked glasses going hazy. They made sure to tune them out after that.

They hiked up steep inclines and navigated narrow ravines, climbing aboard Feathering's back to cross the most difficult terrain. Moreg used her ability to call thunder and lightning to frighten away a snow leopard that none of them had spotted lurking in the shadows, and, when a small avalanche began to roll down a slope towards them, Essential summoned her freezing power to stop the deluge before they passed. It seemed the threats would never cease.

Then, at last, when Willow's legs were sore and her hands and feet numb with cold, they reached an enormous frozen river. The other side was distant and invisible, shrouded in mist.

Lumi held out a hand, and the snowy owl hooted softly. The sky was a frosty blue, the air crisp. He reached out and wrote something in Willow's palm.

The frozen river is the last and worst barrier to the third mountain; many have died trying to cross the ice. You will all face grave danger.

She swallowed, repeating what he'd told her to the others.

'**Oh, me 'orrid aunt,**' muttered Oswin.

Gathering her courage, Willow walked forward and placed her foot on to the frozen lake. A haunting sound came from up ahead through the mist. She lifted her tiny storm light to cast its beam across the river – and REALLY wished she hadn't.

It revealed an army of giants made of thick black ice.

22

The Ice Giants

'Great St-St-Starfell!' whispered Essential as the storm light beamed across the river, illuminating their gigantic shapes, towering twenty feet high. They were made of dirty black ice, and their eyes glowed red.

The ice giants guard the river, ensuring no one gets to the third mountain, said Lumi, writing into Willow's palm. Keep close as I will guide you. But be prepared. Anyone but me who dares to cross makes a declaration.

Willow repeated his words to the group.

'A declaration of what?' asked Moreg.

Willow asked Lumi.

Skadi voiced the chilling answer at the same moment Lumi wrote the word in Willow's palm. 'War.'

Willow swallowed. She didn't know how they'd face

them, but understood they would have to. She met the others' eyes and saw that each one of them seemed to be thinking the same thing.

'Let's go,' she whispered.

Lumi turned and stepped on to the vast frozen river. As Willow and her friends followed him, the ice giants began to make an ear-splitting wailing sound, like a million fingers scratching down a chalkboard.

'Oh, me 'orrid, 'orrid aunt!' screeched Oswin.

And then the enormous beasts began to charge at them.

'All right,' said Feathering, and smoke curled from his nostrils as he began to charge too. Willow watched in awe as he tore straight towards one of the ice giants and butted it with his diamond-hard head.

Lumi took Willow's hand and spelt out the word: Run!

She didn't need telling twice.

Willow and Essential raced behind Skadi, who, in her giant form, used her stone fists to bat away one of the icy behemoths. It yelled, and Willow flinched in fear as she saw its great yellow teeth, like ice picks. It

chilled her to think what teeth like that could do . . .

Then Skadi unsheathed a long sword from a scabbard at her side and plunged it into an ice giant. Its ice body cracked, and it fell to its knees, keeling over.

'Is he dead?' cried Essential as Feathering, ahead, breathed fire over another one, and it began to melt.

Skadi laughed sourly. 'Nope. They never die. They only stop for a few minutes before they begin to re-form. Watch.' She pointed. Soon the giant she'd cut began slowly to piece itself back together. It was like something from a nightmare.

The only way out is to keep fighting. They'll stop coming for you when we've crossed, Lumi explained, writing on Willow's palm.

'Think of it as a bit like weeding,' said Skadi.

As another giant approached them, Essential darted forward to freeze it for a moment, then she dashed behind Skadi again for cover. She continued doing this, using her ability to buy them moments of freedom.

I will try to seek a safe path for you, Lumi wrote, and then he ran ahead of Willow.

Perhaps he could sense the beasts, like he could

sense the Craegun and the mountains, as he sidestepped each giant with apparent ease. As he'd warned, the beasts ignored him; all of their attention was focused on Willow and her friends.

As one of the giants lumbered towards them, Willow tried to run, but slipped. She fell and slid along the frozen river, the hairy carpetbag still clutched in her hand.

An ice giant noticed Willow's moment of weakness and began tearing after her, making that awful, ear-splitting howl. In sheer panic, she scrambled to her feet and banged the carpetbag against its knee. The giant didn't budge; she was like a mouse trying to attack a lion.

Her throat turned dry and, for a horrible moment, as the giant raised a mighty fist, she froze. This was it, she realised. She had no hope . . .

. . . Until the bag opened up and Oswin dived out. He launched himself at the giant, exploding into a fiery ball.

The wave of heat knocked Willow back. It was bigger than any explosion she had seen him have before. The ice giant stumbled away in fear, its edges beginning to melt.

'Brilliant, Oswin!' Willow said from the ground, the open carpetbag in front of her. Then she spied the bottles of potions inside the bag and yelped, 'Of course!'

She took out several. Another enormous ice giant came storming after her and Oswin, and she threw a potion called 'Wait'.

The massive twenty-foot ice giant stopped and blinked at her in surprise with its glowing red eyes.

'Erm, please wait here for today,' she told it. It looked at her and then down at its legs, which were frozen in place by the potion throw, letting out a deep howl of frustration.

Skadi ran by, knocking back another ice giant with her massive fists. 'What's that?' she called.

'Potion throws! They're Granny Flossy's invention.'

'Oh, brilliant!'

But they were both soon distracted, as lightning flashed nearby. They turned and saw Moreg across the river blasting several ice giants all at once.

Willow and Skadi gasped when Moreg turned towards them, raising her hands. It looked for an alarming moment as if she were going to blast *them* – but, when the witch flicked her wrist, the

bolt of lightning struck an ice giant that had been creeping steadily closer to Willow and Skadi while their backs were turned.

Willow let out a breath. 'Thanks!'

'Don't mention it!' yelled Moreg, and she hastened towards them. 'But keep your attention on them. I'll try to get as many as I can. Good thinking with the potion throws,' she added.

At that moment, another ice giant crept a bit too close, and Willow lobbed the bottle labelled 'Sleep' at it.

The giant went crashing, rather satisfyingly, to its knees, and soon there was the sound of heavy snoring thundering round them like a waterfall.

Lightning struck behind Willow. Moreg had gone back into battle.

Feathering flew above, dragging one of the ice giants and flinging it so that it slammed into another one, then raining fire down on them, melting several at once.

Suddenly there was a heart-wrenching scream, and Willow whipped round. Essential had been freezing and dodging the ice giants, but one of them had unfrozen too quickly.

Willow stared in horror as it snatched the young witch in its hands and lifted her high into the air. Essential's scream of terror matched her own.

23

The Jelly Giant

Willow barely had time to think. She ran towards the ice giant as fast as she could. At the last moment, she slipped and skidded along on her bottom – but not before she'd reached into the carpetbag and hurled the potion throw called 'Glamour' at the ice giant's feet.

There was a pause as Willow imagined hard, and she yelled, 'You're made of jelly, not ice!'

The ice giant watched in horror as its arms and legs turned to dark, rubbery jelly.

Essential was able to wriggle free, slipping through its fingers and sliding down its vast jelly body. She bounced off its huge foot and slowed herself down with her magic mid-air before landing, legs splayed, by Willow.

She grinned, her cracked glasses hanging askew. 'Thanks, Willow.'

Then they watched as the jelly-giant tried to wobble towards them, but it didn't get very far at all. Its legs jiggled and bounced, and it sat down with a defeated sigh.

Willow and Essential stood up, but it wasn't over yet.

Another giant came thundering towards them. Willow threw a potion – but it missed, hitting Oswin instead, who had been trying to launch himself at the beast as a glowing fireball.

It was another 'Glamour' throw. Willow thought fast. It wouldn't be good to let it go to waste. 'You're the size of Feathering!' she shouted, just as Essential froze the giant who had dodged the throw.

Oswin swelled up, going from the size of a tabby cat to an enormous cloud dragon, burning all the while like a moving sun.

'NOW this is MORE LIKES IT!' he yelled, throwing himself at the surrounding ice giants. One melted completely and, though it started to re-form slowly from puddle to ice, it was enough to make the others scramble away in haste to escape the flames. Willow grinned – but, unfortunately, she soon realised

Oswin had also begun to melt a patch of the frozen river. A growing pool of water spread over the surface beneath him.

'Watch out, Os!' Willow yelled as she and Essential ran. Their shoes squelched in the melting ice as they tried to stick to solid ground. Still, giants pursued them.

'Let me try,' said Essential, taking a 'Glamour' potion from Willow's bag and throwing it at an ice giant. 'You're a frog!' she said.

This was a mistake.

It was still a GIANT bullfrog – one that croaked and then flicked an enormous tongue towards them, as if they were insects. The tongue hit them with a sticky slap, and it began to drag them along the ice towards the giant frog's open mouth.

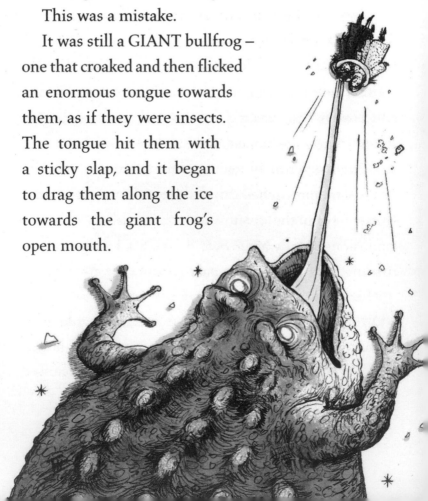

'*AHHHHH!*' they screamed as Essential did her best to slow them down.

Just as they were about to be swallowed, Willow threw another potion, one called '𝕱orget', at the enormous frog. 'Forget you're guarding us from entering the third mountain!' she told it – and they gasped in relief as the frog paused in confusion. It gave them time to rip themselves away from its sticky tongue and escape.

Lumi ran towards Willow. **You're doing well, he** wrote in her palm. **Keep going. We're over halfway there.**

She looked ahead to the other side of the river and saw that he was right. She took heart from this. Except, when she looked in the bag, she saw they were running dangerously low on potion throws.

Oswin approached, no longer aflame, wet and shivery from the river water he'd melted with his explosions. He was growing smaller and smaller, turning once more into a pale green, catlike kobold.

'I is **s–s–spent,**' he said.

Willow picked him up protectively and tucked him back into the carpetbag, where she hoped he might warm up.

She was tired too, and the others were clearly weakening – but there were still so many ice giants blocking their way.

The remaining potions were her last hope. Willow reached into the carpetbag, and threw a bottle on the ground at her own feet. It was 'Strength'. Ox horns grew out of the side of her head, and she felt *alive*.

She threw the other 'Strength' potions at her friends, and they too grew stronger. Essential pawed the ground like a bull before she charged.

Willow spied a small ice pick in a holster near Skadi's knee. 'May I?' she asked.

'Of course. It helps if you think about something or someone that makes you cross.'

For Willow, the pick was like a massive club with a sharp edge, and she grinned. She put the straps of the carpetbag over her shoulders, carrying it at the back, and began to charge at the ice giants herself.

She channelled everything she had been feeling – her guilt, her rage, her feelings of being lost and helpless, her frustration – and clubbed one of the giants hard on the ankle. There was a very satisfying crack, and it began to splinter.

218

There were so many ice giants, though, and they just kept coming.

Willow and her friends fought hard, continually charging towards the other side of the river. As she smashed at the ice giants, steam puffed through her nostrils. But, all too soon, the potion wore off, and Willow was left feeling just as cold and tired as she had before.

She wasn't the only one. Feathering couldn't fly far in the freezing cold, and it was hard for him to keep producing fire. 'I'm out!' he cried, headbutting another giant from his path and joining Willow, Essential and Skadi.

Moreg raced to meet them, giving the giants one last blast of her lightning, but it spluttered and died too.

'Same here,' she said.

They were all exhausted. This, of course, was when the biggest ice giant yet began to stomp towards them. Its eyes glowed red, and in its hand was a long, icy sword.

And it was coming straight for Willow.

24

The Ice Giants' Last Defence

'Run, Willow!' cried Feathering as he launched himself at the giant, trying to muster up some fire, but nothing would come out.

The ice giant batted Feathering away as if he were a fly, and the dragon went skidding across the ice with a yelp.

'No!' cried Willow.

Skadi charged next, her sword raised, roaring as she plunged it into the giant's arm, which broke off.

The giant made that strange chalkboard-scratching sound, and suddenly several other ice giants scurried towards the big one, as if it were their king, and lay down in front of it. The huge ice giant stood on each one of its companions and absorbed them into its own form, growing larger and larger.

'**Oh no,**' Oswin whimpered.

Lumi wrote in Willow's palm: This is a good sign. It is their last defence.

Willow didn't know how to respond to that. Staring up at the mega-giant, she had never seen anything that looked less like a good sign.

You need to topple it.

'What?' Willow cried, repeating what he'd said to the others. 'How?'

But Moreg agreed. 'Look at it the way it's been built, with all those other ice giants. It's top-heavy. If we knock it off balance, its own weight will bring it down. With any luck, that will give us enough time to make it to the other side.'

Skadi nodded. 'You spread out and confuse it! I'll stay close and charge at it.'

'Are you sure, Skadi?' Willow was worried, but the shrink giant nodded bravely, and Willow was sure she grew slightly larger.

Follow me, Lumi wrote into Willow's palm, and, taking her hand, he ran. Essential, Feathering and Moreg split up, scattering in opposite directions.

The enormous ice giant swung round, momentarily confused, unsure which of them to chase. The movement

221

slightly knocked the beast off kilter, and Skadi seized her chance.

She charged at the huge giant and punched it, landing blows that shattered some of its icy body. The beast seemed to lose its balance . . .

'Keep going!' cried Willow as she and the others changed course to make a beeline for the other side of the river.

Skadi went charging at the huge ice giant, landing one final blow. It staggered backwards and began to fall . . .

Willow and the others sprinted to the riverbank – and made it, right as the giant landed with an almighty crash, its head only just missing them. There was a cracking sound, and the surface of the river beneath the giant split.

'Skadi!' Willow cried. How would the shrink giant cross now, with the ice around the giant so precarious?

But Skadi acted quickly, using the fallen giant itself as a bridge to cross over.

Finally, as Skadi leapt from the giant's head to the riverbank, they were all on the other side. They left the frozen river battered and bruised, but saw – to their relief – that they had arrived, at last, at the third mountain.

'We made it,' Willow whispered in disbelief.

25

What Bends but Does Not Break?

Lumi took Willow's hand. There is a cave where we can rest for the night nearby.

Willow told the others what he had said. She wasn't the only one relieved at the thought of stopping for the night. They all looked exhausted, and Feathering couldn't stop sneezing. It sounded like he'd developed a cold.

They followed after Lumi on leaden feet, trudging across the snow-covered ground.

'You were all amazing out there,' Willow said wearily to her friends.

Essential smiled at her. 'So were you.'

Soon they reached a cave entrance, and they came to a grateful halt.

Moreg went ahead and began taking things out

225

from her pantry. The witch looked tired but determined, and before long there was a roaring fire in the corner of the cave, and the smell of something delicious as it began to roast.

Willow shuffled over to lend a hand, but Moreg shook her head. 'You should rest.'

'I don't mind,' said Willow, helping the witch as she brought out several large cushions to sit on, plates, knives and forks and some large flagons of water. Two were bigger than Oswin, and she handed these to Skadi and Feathering, who drank from them thirstily.

While Willow sat before the fire, enjoying a plate of bearfrost soup and krim rice, which was hearty and delicious, Lumi came to sit next to her. He had a plate filled with frozen berries balanced on his knee and popped several into his mouth. After they'd both almost finished, he tapped Willow on the shoulder and explained what would happen in the morning.

Tomorrow your trials will begin, he wrote into her palm. I will be your guide, but you will have to face them alone. Your friends will not be able to help.

Willow swallowed, then nodded, reporting back to the others. There were several cries and gasps.

'Not **even** me?' cried Oswin. '**I mean, we** is never

226

apart.' This was true, and it made Willow's heart ache until he added, **"cept from when we goes ter the privy.'**

The others laughed, but their hearts weren't in it.

Moreg touched Willow's shoulder. 'Not even I can help you. I've been trying . . . Sometimes, if I concentrate, I can get glimpses of a future I'm focused on, but with you there has been nothing. He's making sure that I can't see.'

'I think it's unfair,' said Essential. 'Look at Willow – she's dead on her feet.'

'I'll be all right,' said Willow, gazing round at her friends and feeling moved, and loved. 'You all make me strong.'

'Oh, Willow,' said Essential, and she bit her lip, like she didn't want to cry. 'You know I can't believe that the ice giants weren't even part of the Craegun's test . . .' Essential broke off, but her unspoken words were loud: what horrors lay in store for Willow if those were only the guardians to the beginning of her trials?

It was Moreg who, as ever, took charge, suggesting they all get an early night, handing round the same purple sleeping bags they had used the day before.

Willow was sure that she wouldn't be able to sleep for worrying, but she was so bodily tired that, almost

227

as soon as she lay down, she drifted off into a fitful sleep. She tossed and turned, dreaming of frost, ice giants and sick trees, moaning in her sleep.

In the early hours of the morning, as the wind howled outside the cave, Willow woke with a start. Her heart was racing inside her chest. She was freezing cold and shivering, and inside her palm was the iron half-moon.

She looked at it with a frown. When she glanced around, she saw that everyone else was asleep, but the small storm light was still glowing beside her, where she'd left it. She opened the hairy carpetbag and took out the notebook, like she had the morning before, to find comfort in Granny Flossy's words.

But the next entry made her heart start to clap like thunder.

Deep below the mountains, we heard a rumble. The frost child told me that sometimes the beast turns in its slumber. He says that the beast will only awaken for someone who is strong enough to withstand what it can offer. So far, very few have.

Willow swallowed.

Her eyes stared at the words Granny Flossy had written: 'strong enough'.

She knew this, but seeing it there in black and white made Willow pause, doubts swarming over her like ants, ready and willing to bite.

She didn't feel strong. She felt exhausted – bone-tired and chilled to the core. She started to cough, and it was a loud, wrenching sound that shook her whole body. She sighed. They'd already been through so much, and she still had to face the Craegun – and then, if she somehow managed that, confront Silas too.

She felt a cold hand reach for her and started. It was Lumi.

Willow, he wrote in her palm.

Yes, she replied, not understanding.

He shook his finger – no. Then took her hand again and began to draw in it. Inside her palm, something made out of frost and magic began to grow. It was a willow tree, small, with beautiful weeping branches.

Willow gasped as she stared at it.

Lumi took her other palm and wrote inside that: **Strong.**

She didn't know how he knew what she was feeling.

229

Perhaps he could sense it somehow, the way he sensed the Craegun.

Willow shook her head. Then she wrote into his hand: **Willows aren't strong.**

He smiled at her. Yes, they are. It's a good name. Chosen with love.

Willow stared. **My granny named me**.

To her surprise, he nodded. I know. She told me about you when she lived here.

Willow blinked. **She did?**

Yes.

She felt something catch inside her throat.

A memory floated up, unbidden.

She was seven and begging her older sisters to take her with them to the market.

'Fine,' said Camille. 'You can come – just go inside and fetch me my wrap. We'll wait for you in the garden.'

Willow raced inside, tore into the room she shared with Camille, and then came rushing back with the wrap – only to stop mid-stride as she watched them jump the low wall and run away, laughing. Tears filled her eyes.

Granny Flossy, who had seen and heard it all from the greenhouse nearby, called out to her. 'We'll go together, child. Don't mind them.'

Willow looked away, wiping her eyes.

Willow and Granny Flossy took the long way to the market, along the riverbank where the weeping willows grew.

'Did you know it was me that named you?' asked Granny Flossy.

'You named me?' Willow blinked. 'Why "Willow"?' She looked at the willow trees along the banks. 'I'm not tall...'

'It's not about height – it's a name that reflects who I saw inside. The willow isn't as mighty as the oak or as impervious as a hawthorn, and it can be big or small, but what sets it apart is the fact that it bends, but does not break. It is a quiet strength that is inside you, like your namesake.'

Willow swallowed. She hadn't thought of that in years.

Be the willow, Lumi wrote on her palm, and she closed her hand over his words, as if to hold on to them for a while.

26

The Trial Begins

At dawn, Willow sat up – only to glance round in panic.

She was alone. The others had vanished, and so had the hairy carpetbag. What had happened to everyone?

She picked up Granny's notebook and put it in the pocket of her dress before slipping on her coat and shoes and racing to the mouth of the cave.

Lumi stood there, pale and glittering in the bright daylight. He turned his blind eyes towards her, then nodded, beckoning her to follow. Finally, Willow understood. It was the start of her test. That was why she was suddenly alone.

She followed Lumi, who darted lightly across the frozen ground, and together they began to climb the third mountain.

*

They climbed and climbed.

Soon Willow was chilled to the bone and thirsty. The wind was battering her skin, and her lips became chapped and sore.

At last, Lumi stopped climbing, and so did Willow, with some relief. She was grateful to be resting, even if just for a moment. But then she cried out in alarm when, suddenly, he was gone. Heart hammering, she peered round the jagged rocks, trying to find him, but he had vanished completely.

After some time, she realised there was nothing else to do. She had to keep going without him. So, though every step was difficult, she began to climb once more.

She hadn't taken her tonic that morning, and she could feel how shattered she was from the day before, her limbs bruised, her muscles aching. The blizzard had stopped, and all Willow could see were miles of white-capped mountains, utterly desolate and empty.

For a moment, she desperately wanted to cry. Every step she took, her feet were like lead, and she felt completely alone. But she didn't cry. Instead, she pictured Twist's face and closed her eyes tightly. 'I can

233

be strong. One step more,' she told herself, again and again.

Willow licked her lips. Her throat was dry and parched, so she reached for the snow on the ground, picked up a small pile and ate some. It tasted like the most delicious thing she could ever recall. She sighed with relief and ate some more. Then she kept on climbing.

After several hours, she felt hunger pangs, which she tried her best to ignore. But, as the day wore on and the morning turned to afternoon, she was beginning to feel faint. As her hands grasped the rocks, she spied some frost-covered berries, and saliva pooled in her mouth.

She sat on a tiny ledge and picked a handful, but she didn't know if they were safe or not. She held one up to her nose and sniffed. It didn't have a scent. She put it in her lap and placed her head in her hands. She wanted Nolin Sometimes or Granny Flossy. They would know what was safe and what wasn't. All she needed now was to try the berries and get poisoned . . .

She was weak. Tired. This was meant to be some kind of test, and all Willow felt was lost and afraid and unsure of herself. She couldn't remember ever feeling

234

this alone before. Or this helpless.

What if she died out here? What if she never managed to get to the top of the mountain? She didn't have anything with her – no food, no water, no ropes or anything really.

She closed her eyes, then concentrated on breathing in and out, breathing in to the count of six, holding it and releasing it to the same count. It was a technique her friend Sprig, a boy who could turn into a raven, had taught her once. When Willow's anxiety had grown larger than she could handle after Granny Flossy had died and her magic started misfiring, he'd shown her how to calm her heartrate down through her breathing.

She repeated the breaths until whatever beast had decided to make a home inside her belly finally sheathed its claws. Thinking of Sprig had calmed her down. It was like he was sitting there before her now – and, for a moment, she thought she *saw* him, in his raven form, circling above before flying behind a rocky peak.

She gasped. Was it him, or had her mind simply conjured up the image? She didn't know, but she felt buoyed by it.

Then Willow realised that, although she didn't have many provisions with her, she did have something important. She pulled out Granny Flossy's notebook, thinking about the things her grandmother had drawn and written. Perhaps there was something in there that Willow would recognise out here, something that might be edible . . .

She flipped through the pages until she came to a page that contained drawings of an assortment of odd mushrooms. None of them were native to the mountains of Nach, but it sparked something inside Willow's mind nonetheless.

A memory floated into her mind of a time when she was seven, and she was walking in the woods with her sisters and Granny Flossy.

Granny picked up an odd green mushroom and frowned. 'Never seen one of these before,' she said. Then, before their eyes, she placed it under her armpit and carried on walking.

Camille and Juniper shared a look of utter bemusement and began to giggle behind their hands. There was

a group of girls from their village up ahead, and Willow's sisters started to walk faster in front of Granny Flossy, as if they were pretending she wasn't with them.

Willow crept up to Granny and slipped her hand into hers. 'Why did you put that mushroom under your armpit?' she asked. 'Was it to keep it safe?'

Granny Flossy grinned. 'Oh no, it was to keep us safe.'

Willow frowned, confused, so Granny explained.

'See, under the arm is the most sensitive part of the body — at least one of them anyway. So if I was going to get a reaction from these mushrooms, if they were poisonous, I'd know about it here first, see. If I don't, they're probably safe to eat.'

'Oh well, that makes sense,' said Willow.

'It does. But I bet it looked really strange when I did it at first?'

Willow nodded. 'Very.'

'So how come you didn't walk ahead like your sisters? Why did you come and ask?'

Willow thought about it for a long while, then said, 'Because there's usually a reason for something odd. Well, at least the things you do. It might look

weird at first – like how you stop by the wall and tap one of the cracks three times just before you enter the house – but there's a reason.'

Granny looked amused. 'When did you notice that there was a reason for that?'

'A few weeks ago. It's to warn the Glignels we're home, isn't it?'

Glignels were tiny creatures who were very hairy and had short little horns and stocky bodies, and they liked nothing better than burrowing into walls and stealing house scraps – mostly used teabags and the mould from cheese and that sort of thing.

'Yep. Your mum has threatened to bring in an exterminator if she ever catches them, so I like to give them a chance to hide. They're grateful too. Every so often, I find a present in return. I mean, they're usually disgusting, if I'm honest – things that have rolled beneath beds and carpets and grown mould, like apple cores, and once half a dead mouse, but their hearts are in the right place.'

The two laughed.

Granny looked at Willow with narrowed eyes and asked, 'And what if there hadn't been a purpose to what I did with the mushroom?'

'Well,' said Willow, thinking seriously, 'then it would have been even more of a reason not to run away from you, because then I'd have known you'd lost your marbles.'

And the two started to cackle loudly, making Willow's sisters walk even faster – which set them off even more.

Willow smiled and put one of the berries she'd found under her arm.

Then, just as she was sure she'd spotted Sprig, for a moment she was convinced she caught a glimpse of Granny Flossy walking ahead. She seemed to turn back and wink at her before disappearing again.

Willow felt tears smart her eyes, but she couldn't help grinning. Perhaps she wasn't as alone as she thought.

Feeling brighter, she carried on climbing, putting the bunch of berries in her pocket. After half an hour, she took out the one she'd placed under her arm. Nothing had happened. She gave it a little lick, then kept going, kept walking. Twenty minutes later, she still didn't feel any reaction, so she took a tiny nibble and waited some more. Her stomach growled in hunger. She had to resist shoving them all into her mouth, but after another twenty minutes at last, she said, 'Here goes,' and ate one. It tasted a bit like vanilla and ice, and she carried on eating them. By the time she was done, she almost felt like herself again.

Soon Willow came to a herd of yaks, with their thick winter coats, grazing on the side of the mountain. She noticed one in the distance with what looked like green freckles and paused. She'd seen that before, hadn't she?

Then she opened up Granny's notebook and flicked through the pages, stopping at the splotchy one that was wrinkled from Granny's tears – the day she'd made the 'Forget' potion and it had accidentally spilled on to her beloved yak.

There was the drawing of the large yak with long, thick hair the colour of chestnuts. He had huge horns and, yes, he was flecked with green all over.

Willow stopped. 'Ed?' she called.

For just a moment, the yak stopping chewing and looked up at her. He stared, as if perhaps he recognised something in her too.

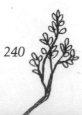

Willow smiled, and in that exact moment Lumi reappeared. He stepped to the side, and suddenly, turning away from the yaks, Willow saw she was at the top of the third mountain.

Willow approached Lumi and wrote into his palm: **Was that one of my tests?**

It was hard, but it hadn't been impossible.

He nodded. At the start of the trial, you were sure you couldn't do this alone. You have faced the harshness of the mountain without magic, using only your wits, and you have survived. It might seem a simple task, but it is not easy to keep a cool head out here. Very often, people forget how to think when emotions take over. But you calmed yourself, and you used all you knew, and in doing so you realised that you are never truly alone. We all carry a part of the people who came before us. That is how we go forward, and how we survive. There will be two more challenges. Then he faded away once more.

'Wait!' cried Willow, but he was already gone.

In his place was a woman. Or what might have been one a long time ago.

27

The Second Trial

The woman was tall and thin, with pale, translucent white skin and long black hair. She had horns on either side of her head and cherry-red lips.

As she moved towards Willow, the landscape around them began to change, and the mountain became shrouded in mist.

Willow stared. Was this the spirit woman her grandmother had mentioned?

'Walaika?' she breathed.

The spirit woman bowed

and put her palms together. Then she beckoned Willow forward and Willow approached reluctantly.

Walaika's face looked sad for a moment as she waved her palms towards the sky, as if she were scrubbing it clear, and suddenly everything around Willow changed.

The mountain vanished, and Walaika disappeared like a plume of smoke.

Instead, Willow was in a forest full of dying trees, their bark blackened. Faces appeared in their rotten trunks, crumpled with pain. Their eyes seemed to bore into her own. There was a low hissing sound, and she walked nervously forward, feeling her heart thundering in her chest.

Moments ago, this forest hadn't been here, but it seemed so real. The forest was in pain, and, as she walked, she felt it too – and something more. It began to grow inside her, along with the strange, spine-tingling hissing: a feeling of not being welcome. At every twist and every turn, the trees turned away from her, their blackened bark cold, stiff and unwelcoming.

Willow swallowed, her throat turning dry. Then, up ahead, she saw something that made her come to a screeching halt.

It dominated the forest – a tree so large it was the

size of several farmhouses
stacked on top of one
another. It winked blue in
the dim light, then, before
her eyes, it began to turn
black.

Willow gasped. 'No!'
she cried.

A giant face appeared
in the bark of the Great
Wisperia Tree, like an
old man with bushy
eyebrows, craggy skin
and eyes as sharp as flint.
It was a face so real she
almost recognised it. The
way it glared at her made
her flinch.

She hesitated, then
stepped forward, wanting,
needing to make the tree
stop looking at her like that.

'Get away from us,' it
hissed.

Willow halted, her heart catching in her throat. 'No, please, I can help you.'

'You? Haven't you done enough? The forest is dying because of you,' it hissed in a low voice.

Willow blinked. Tears pooled in her eyes.

'Magic was wrong to trust you. It should have picked someone else, someone stronger . . .'

Willow felt as if the air had been punched out of her lungs.

'You tricked it into believing in you,' the Great Wisperia Tree spat. 'You wanted us to think you were special.'

'No!' said Willow. 'I didn't, I promise. I . . . I just wanted to help.'

She felt like she might shatter from the sharpness of its flinty eyes.

'Help?' said the tree, its shrivelled skin folding into a sneer. 'How did you help us? You brought the elf staff back into the world and ensured that magic would suffer. Why did you do that, Willow? Why?'

Then the face changed, the anger giving way to a horrible sadness.

'We chose you. We put our faith in you and look what you did to us.' The face in the Great Wisperia

246

Tree crumpled, and it looked like a sad old man. It broke Willow's heart.

'I'm sorry! I'm so sorry,' she cried, falling to her knees. 'I never meant for that to happen, I promise. I will try to fix it, try to help you.'

'How can you? Look what you've already done to us. How can we ever trust you again? You wanted so much to feel special like your sisters, to be someone of importance – to prove that you were just as good. You risked *everything* for your vanity. You were selfish and reckless and weak. That's why your family always left you alone, why your parents are ashamed of you, and why your sisters always used to run away from you. Silas saw it too. You're not good enough, Willow. We should have seen it as well.'

Tears were falling hard and fast. Willow sat on the forest floor and hugged her knees, struggling to catch her breath past the pain in her heart. Everything the tree said brought to life her very worst fears, the worst things she'd ever thought about herself and her life.

She swallowed, clenching her fists. Then, in a quiet corner of her mind, her own voice said, *Fears are not facts.*

She blinked. *Fears.* That's what this was! This was

Walaika. She hadn't disappeared – she was showing Willow her worst fears realised, just as she'd shown Granny. This was what Willow dreaded most – that magic had been wrong to put its faith in her. That she wasn't enough.

She dashed the tears from her eyes and then stood up on trembling limbs.

This wasn't right. This wasn't the Great Tree. It would never say such things. It was old, and wise, and kind . . . and it believed in her, even when she did not.

'You're not the Great Wisperia Tree,' she whispered, finding her courage as she did so. 'It wouldn't say this to me. It would know that I was only trying my best. I didn't think I was special, and I still don't. All I ever wanted to do was help. Yes, perhaps there's a bit of vanity in that, in its own way, because it makes me feel good to help, but I don't think it's a bad thing to want to make a difference. Yes, I can be reckless, but that's only because I *care*. I care A LOT and that's why I try. And why I'll keep trying.

'My parents are not ashamed of me. *I* was the one who felt ashamed for having what I thought was a weak magical ability. But now I don't feel that way. I might not have had the most powerful magic, the flashiest,

248

the one everyone spoke about – and yes, for a long, long time that did bother me. But it doesn't any more.

'Because while I might never look like my sisters, or have an ability like theirs, they'll never be like *me*. It's taken a long time, but I finally *like* who I am. I'm kind, and a good friend, and whenever anyone needs me I'm there. It's not flashy or glamorous, but it's what makes me Willow Moss.

'I'm sorry that I failed, that I didn't manage to protect Starfell, and Silas got the elf staff, but I won't let him use it. I'm going to keep trying to stop him. Because I *am* good enough. I'm the girl who says yes when her friends need help. Magic wasn't wrong to trust me,' she promised. 'I will never give up.'

Suddenly the forest scene before her began to fade, like ashes in the wind, and Willow found herself back on top of the third mountain.

Walaika smiled and she bowed again. 'Well done,' she said. 'You are ready to face your final trial.'

28

The Final Trial

Walaika held out her hands, and suddenly the sky began to dance with light in shades of green and purple. The dancing aurora appeared to stretch towards Walaika, as if it were a partner holding out its hands at the start of a waltz.

Willow gasped in awe as the lights reached for them.

Walaika stood on tiptoe, and then with one hand she grasped a gambolling strand of purple, and with the other a strand of green, and she began to knit the light together as if it were yarn. The moving aurora soon formed a vast bridge in front of Walaika, starting at her feet.

'You must take the aurora bridge to the next mountain,' said Walaika.

For a moment, Willow could only stare in astonishment at what she'd just seen. Then Lumi appeared midway across the bridge, and he beckoned for her to follow him.

Willow climbed on to the bridge, her legs still a little trembly. She felt emotionally wrung-out from everything that had already happened, but she knew she had to keep going. The aurora moved beneath her feet like a gentle river, but somehow it carried her across to the next mountain. From so high above, Willow could see the vast peaks of the mountains, the snow, and the dips and valleys beneath. It was beautiful. In front of her was a large cave, and Lumi was waiting outside. He beckoned once more for her to follow.

Willow entered the mouth of the cave and felt the air grow even colder. It was sharp and icy as she breathed in, inching forward into a deep, dark cavern. For a moment, she couldn't see anything.

'H-hello,' she called, and the sound reverberated across the walls, coming back to her in echoes: *H-hello-hello-ello.*

Willow's vision began at last to adjust, and what she saw was a deep grey cave, filled with a dim light, where something above her appeared to move and glitter like diamonds. She looked up at it, only to cry out in alarm as several large, pointed icicles began to fall from the cave ceiling. These were the glittering things, she realised.

'What on Starfell!' she screeched and began to run, dodging the falling icicles, weaving from side to side.

She yelped as one of them grazed her arm, tearing her coat. She managed to roll away as another sharp icicle came falling down. She scrambled to the back wall of the cave, rubbing her arm where the shard of ice had scraped her. The hole in her clothes went through to her skin, and she could see a scratch, but it wasn't bleeding too badly.

Suddenly the ground began to shake, like there was an earthquake. Rocks and other debris started to roll towards her, and she ran back the way she had come to get out of the way once more – but she stumbled, and her foot got stuck inside a small crevice. She tried to pull it out, but it wouldn't budge.

In mounting desperation, Willow pulled and pulled, but nothing happened. She felt a huge wave of fatigue almost engulf her. She couldn't help wishing for all this to be over . . .

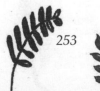

But then she started to get *angry*. This wasn't how it was meant to happen. Hadn't she passed two challenges already on the third mountain, not to mention everything that came before – on the second mountain, the ice giants? How could she be stopped now by something so stupid, so small?

'I have something I need to do!' she yelled, clenching her fists.

It wasn't fair. It couldn't be over when she was so close! The injustice roiled inside her like a spitting thing, until something Granny told her once floated in her mind. *'Life is many things, my child – wonderful, mysterious, hard, sometimes inexplicable – but it isn't fair.'*

Willow paused. *Life wasn't fair.*

Granny was right. The people we loved died. People who only thought about their own lives, their own desires – like Silas – sometimes won. She thought of Moreg. The most powerful people we knew could falter just when we needed them to be strong.

That was life. But it didn't mean you stopped loving people in case you lost them, or forgot them just because it hurt to remember. It didn't mean you gave up just because someone had outsmarted you. You tried again. And when the people you trusted weren't strong when you needed them to be? Well, that was when you found the strength inside yourself to be strong for both of you.

Willow bent over and unknotted the laces of her shoe. Then she wiggled and pulled her leg until her foot, at last, reappeared. There were holes in her sock, and her skin was red and chafed and sore, but she was free.

Lumi appeared before her, and he looked worried. He rushed towards her and took her hand.

Oh no, Willow, he wrote. You're injured. You can't carry on now.

Willow frowned. **Yes, I can,** she wrote back.

There was a gust of wind as if something huge were sighing. Then the rumbling resumed, and the walls began to cave in. Giant rocks were crashing down everywhere.

Come on, wrote Lumi urgently. I'll get you out of there. We can turn back.

Willow hesitated, then jumped away from a falling boulder that nearly landed on her head. Her heart was thundering inside her chest. Lumi wasn't meant to help her . . .

She blinked. This was still part of the test.

Because that was like life – it tested you and didn't

stop. You found out who you were when times were hard. That was when you needed to stick to who you wanted to be most.

Willow was cold, she was tired and in pain. She wanted nothing more than to lie down and let someone else, *anyone* else, take charge. So now she had to dig deepest for her courage.

She swallowed and wrote back: **No! I am going to carry on!**

She would be the willow tree she was named after. She would bend, but she would *not* break.

Then she dived out of the way of another falling rock and landed hard on her forearms. She yelled at the cave, at the Craegun and, at this point, life itself.

'I'm not going back! Not until I make a bargain with you, Craegun, and get my magic back so that I can save Starfell!'

She stood up again and shouted,

'So you can keep throwing things at me,
keep showing me my worst fears and making
me feel like I'm all alone – that's fine;
do what you have to do –
but if there's a chance I can save my friend,
if there's a chance I can save Starfell,
I'm not giving up.'

Suddenly everything turned quiet. The cave stopped
trembling, and the rocks stilled. Lumi disappeared.

A very dry, ancient voice greeted Willow.

'Well, that's promising.'

29

The Craegun

There was the scent of something old, as if Willow were smelling time itself. She turned round and blinked.

Where there had been nothing before was a dragon. An ice dragon. He was as big as the cave itself, his skin made of ice and snow. He glittered like a jewel. 'You wish to make a bargain with me?' he said.

This was the Craegun, Willow realised. Finally, her moment had come. To her surprise, despite everything she'd faced, her voice rang out clearly.

'I need to stop someone who is trying to destroy Starfell. He stole my magic, and he plans on doing the same to everyone else. He has become powerful, and dangerous, and though I didn't mean to I played a part in that – helping him to acquire an ancient, dangerous

magic known as the elf staff, which has been causing harm to our world. I need my magic back so I can take the staff away from him.'

There was a pause as the Craegun absorbed her words. In the silence, all Willow could hear was the sound of her own heart thudding.

Then the Craegun spoke. 'I have felt what you speak of – this destruction. It is creeping to the edges of my mountains, growing closer, and Magic, I know, has led you to me . . . It trusts you, which is a great honour, but I can see it is also a great responsibility – one you have borne with much courage in facing these trials.

'I almost wish that I could break the rules and restore what was taken from you without a price. But I cannot. I am but a part of Starfell, and, as you have seen, its great beating heart is breaking. It is breaking because the balance of magic has been upset once more.

'The elf staff should not have been created. Magic, you see, was never supposed to be controlled like this. It was meant to give itself freely, to run in the rivers, grow in the forests, chase the seas. It should never have been distilled as it was – and crafted into

a weapon. The power of the staff must come from somewhere, and it is being channelled from the heart of Starfell. The one who wields it is using this magic without giving back.

'So I cannot give without taking something away. This is balance, you see, like the way summer must always give way to autumn, and winter to spring, each cycle fuelling the next. I cannot create something from nothing.'

Willow thought of Lumi's mother giving up her magic to the Craegun. 'But I . . . I have no magic to pay you with,' she said, her voice trembling.

'Alas, this is true.'

'Please – can't I give you something else? I'd give anything to have my magic back.'

The Craegun shook his head. 'You must understand that in any case I could not give you back the magic that was stolen from you. *Your* magic is trapped within the elf staff.'

'W-what do you mean? I . . . I thought you could restore lost things—?'

The Craegun interrupted. 'My power differs from yours. You would never truly have *your* magic back, just like your friend Lumi did not return to

261

his previous life, but was reborn from his mother's magic.'

Willow felt something sink inside her. 'Can you help me? At all?'

'There is one thing I can do for you, Willow. I can grant you the abilities you have lost by taking some of the magic of Starfell and giving it, temporarily, to you. I may only do this because magic trusts you and will allow this small gift. But it is a borrowed thing. The magic I lend you will return to Starfell after you have used your power just once.'

Willow paused, feeling both relief and sorrow wash through her. 'I . . . I will be able to find lost things again – or make them disappear – but only once?'

'Yes.'

Willow swallowed, then nodded.

'This is my bargain,' said the beast. 'I'm sorry that I cannot give you more.'

Despite her own grief, Willow understood. 'If you did, Starfell would only suffer more.'

If this was how she felt with her magic drained from her, she could only imagine the agony Starfell was suffering.

'To begin, look into my eyes,' said the Craegun.

262

Willow did. Inside them she saw pain, death, chaos, destruction . . . Starfell dying. She blinked, but instinctively she knew she wasn't to look away. She gritted her teeth and told herself to *bend*. And she did.

In his eyes, she saw, at last, only herself – a girl with eyes that turned up at the corners and long brown hair. She had a kind face, she realised, and for a moment she smiled, as if she were recognising a friend.

The ice dragon looked impressed. 'It is some years since I have found a soul worthy. It is sometimes the greatest triumph to face oneself and come up victorious – to see past the darkness to the light.' The Craegun considered her. 'Tell me why I shouldn't stop this war myself.'

Willow looked at him. For a moment, she didn't have an answer. He could, couldn't he? Just rise up and take out Silas himself? But then she thought about his words.

The great Craegun didn't actually have his own store of power. He exchanged it – he used one source of magic to create something else. But, if he used magic to go after Silas, he wouldn't be *exchanging* anything:

he would be using something . . . something that was already starting to run out. Willow's own power was small, but even giving her that amount of magic would hurt Starfell. Magic had broken the rules before to help her, and now it was taking another chance so that she could help it.

'Because if you did, even though you would be trying to help, you could destroy Starfell by further upsetting the balance.'

'Yes,' he breathed. He sounded pleased. 'You will only have one chance to get the staff. Good luck, Willow.'

'Thank you,' she said.

'One more thing. If you succeed, and the staff is yours, you will have a choice. Only you will be able to make it, and it must be made freely.'

'What choice?' she asked.

'You will find out when the time comes.'

Willow nodded.

Then the Craegun breathed on her, and thousands of tiny snowflakes were exhaled from his mouth, covering her. Willow gasped, but it wasn't from cold. It felt cool and tingly. The snowflakes began to melt into her skin, until suddenly the fatigue

she'd felt for so long miraculously dissolved.

She blinked, and she could feel it.

Magic, flowing through her body once more.

30

Leaving the Mountains

Willow exited the cave, and Lumi was waiting for her outside. Night had fallen. Behind him was the aurora bridge. He beckoned for her to follow, and she did.

The bridge of cascading light carried them across the sky, all the way back down to the foot of the third mountain, where she found her friends. They cheered as she approached.

Feathering yelled, 'You got your magic?'

Willow stepped from the aurora bridge back on to the snowy ground and nodded. She knew then, after everything they'd done, there was no way she could tell them that it was only on loan. They might not understand.

The cloud dragon reared up on his hind legs.

'Marvellous news!'

'Well done,' cried Skadi, banging the end of her sword on the ground.

Essential clapped her hands together, eyes shining in delight.

Oswin raced towards her and dived into her arms. He looked brighter, more like his normal self.

Willow hugged him, and she swallowed. It was for the best not to tell them about the bargain. It didn't matter, not really. It mattered that she could help – that she might be able to save Starfell. Then she smiled, and it was real, because yes, the price was dear, but so was the reward – there was the chance that she could save them all.

Moreg looked at her for a long moment, and for a second Willow was sure that the witch truly could read minds, but then she pulled her into a big hug and said, 'I am so proud of you, Willow.'

Willow grinned. 'Thank you, but after all that we still need to actually face Silas. It's hard to believe anything will be worse than the Craegun's tests, but . . .'

'That likely will be,' she agreed. Then she frowned and looked down at Willow's feet. She was only

267

wearing one shoe – her other was still stuck inside the Craegun's cave. 'Hang on,' said Moreg, and started to rummage in her portal cloak. She brought out a pair of furry boot slippers. 'Better than nothing.'

Willow took them from her gratefully and put them on. When she looked up, she seemed tired but determined. 'We need to get to the fortress of Wolkana.'

'Not a moment too soon,' agreed Feathering. 'Look.' He nodded his head towards the sky, where both of Starfell's moons were partially obscured behind a cloud. They were slowing turning faintly green. 'By the time we get there tomorrow morning, it will be the start of the greening moon.'

Willow took a breath. Tomorrow Silas would be able to perform the ritual using Twist's blood and create a new iron half-moon.

Essential handed Willow her hairy carpetbag and Oswin leapt inside.

'We will follow you there shortly,' said Skadi.

'You're coming?' asked Willow.

'Of course. I will bring Lumi. We are going to ask the other giants to come too.'

Lumi came forward, touched her hand and wrote:

This is your fight, but we must all help you win.

She clasped his hand in response, then she, Essential and Moreg climbed on to Feathering's back. The dragon took a running leap and then launched himself at the sky.

They travelled over the mountains as the stars winked like pinpricks in the darkness.

While Feathering flew, Moreg handed round dried fruit and meat and a large flagon of water. Though simple fare, it was delicious.

Willow touched the iron half-moon in her pocket and, strapped securely to Feathering, fell into a dreamless sleep beside Essential. Tonight the dragon made no stops, pushing on, even through his own fatigue. At dawn, they were just approaching the outskirts of Wolkana.

Willow and the others could see the toll the war that had been waged against the Brothers of Wol had taken. The area surrounding the fortress looked charred and barren. It was filled with people and magical creatures who, even at first light, were all fighting.

Willow spotted the Howling aunts moving like

tornadoes against a band of Brothers, who appeared to have been drawn into battle away from the fortress, rain and thunder pouring out of their open mouths.

Non-magical people were fighting witches and wizards. She heard one man cry out, 'When the Brothers of Wol are victorious, your magic will be drained! Then we will all know peace at last!'

There were several cries and cheers.

'No!' cried another voice.

Willow saw her non-magical friend, Peg, and his mother bustling their way to the front.

'Don't be fools,' said Peg. 'They have done you no harm! This is what Silas wants – he wants to make you believe that we are on opposite sides. We aren't! Silas isn't stealing magic to rid it from the world – he wants to keep it and make himself powerful, turn himself into a god!'

'Nonsense, what nonsense,' scoffed several people.

Feathering flew on. Closer to the fortress there was more fighting – rock dragons battling trolls.

Willow spotted her troll friend, Calamity, and a band of dwarfs deep in discussion.

Up in the sky, she saw a flock of ravens. At the front was one with a smoky blue wing, who she was sure

was her friend Sprig. The ravens were dive-bombing the Brothers.

Still they flew on and Willow saw her family deep in the fray. Her mother and father were speaking seriously to some non-magical folk. Perhaps they were trying to change people's minds, make them see that it was possible to live side by side.

Up ahead, Juniper was using her abilities in an attempt to blast the ground around the fortress, but nothing was budging. Camille was moving large boulders with her mind, placing them in front of the non-magical people who were trying to capture witches and wizards without active powers like her own. Willow felt proud of them.

Rubix was controlling several suits of armour that were beginning to snatch at some of the Brothers too, while officials from the Enchancil were preparing to launch magical canons at the walls. They were all fighting valiantly, but they were getting nowhere.

Willow looked up and saw that the moons were turning ever greener. Soon they would be fully green, and then it would be too late.

Finally, Feathering came in to land, and Willow and her friends climbed down.

271

'You can do this, Willow,' said Feathering.

'Yes,' said Essential, giving her hand a squeeze.

Willow nodded. She had one chance to use her magic.

One chance to save Twist.

One last chance to save Starfell.

She began to walk towards the high walls of the fortress. Then she took out the small, glittering iron half-moon from her pocket – and she raised it high above her head.

31

The Battle Cry

There was a sound like the sky splitting in two as Moreg raised a hand to the heavens to call down a deafening boom of thunder. A shocked silence ensued as magical and non-magical folk turned to see the cause.

'Silas!' Willow yelled into the quiet. 'I have brought you the iron half-moon!'

Nothing happened. The huge gate inside the wall remained closed. Behind her, she heard hurried footsteps. She turned to see her parents running towards her, and her sisters too.

There was an ear-splitting cry and Sprig appeared, turning from a raven into a boy.

'We'll keep the Brothers away. Tell me you know what you're doing,' he said.

'I do.'

The huge gate began, at last, to creak open. Silas came striding out of the fortress, the elf staff clutched in his hands.

As he neared, he said, 'So you are here at last.' He shook his head and gave her a magnanimous yet condescending smile, speaking to her as if she were very young. 'All of this could have been avoided if you'd come sooner. But no matter. You're here now.'

Willow realised that he didn't look so fearsome to her any more, or as strong. He looked like a young boy trying desperately to be the worst version of what it meant to be strong. Silas held out his hand and tried to summon the iron half-moon. But, of course, thanks to the wispdust, it did not come.

'I see you are using some kind of magical protection. So it's a bargain you want – your friend in exchange?'

Willow held her breath and nodded. They *needed* Twist to be out of the fortress so that one of them could get her away safely. 'Yes, that's right. The iron half-moon in exchange for Twist.'

He sneered, then made to step closer to Willow, as if he would simply snatch it from her, but Moreg sent a warning blast of lightning that tore from the sky.

Silas shrugged. 'I see you are serious about your

request. Well, I will not waste time fighting. The elf girl is of no use to me if I can have the original iron half-moon.'

He snapped his fingers and a pair of Brothers were summoned from within the fortress. They stepped out through the gate, holding on to Twist, who was struggling against a pair of glowing manacles. Her clothes were dirty and torn, and her white hair, usually windswept, was limp. Something grey swirled round her like dirty smoke. It was the north wind, Skiron, Willow realised, and it looked ill.

Willow's heart lurched. 'Oh, Twist,' she breathed. She turned back to the wizard. 'You don't have to do any of this, Silas. Look at what's happening around you – the division, the pain. Starfell is suffering. It's dying. It's not too late to just embrace who you are. There's nothing wrong with having magic.'

A muscle twitched above his eye. 'The iron half-moon,' he said tightly, holding out a hand.

Willow carried on, stepping forward. 'I know what it's like to feel ashamed. I was never the one with the strongest powers in my family, and for a long time that made me feel bad. But I've found that there is another kind of strength – it's finding the courage to be proud of the gifts you were given, to be tolerant when others aren't, and to be kind in a world that doesn't reward it. Strength is not letting your heart harden just because it's easier than letting it become bruised or broken by hope or love. It's accepting who you are, even the dark, strange parts. It's not too late for you.'

Silas made a scoffing sound – only to then blink in surprise as the spirit hare, Molsa, appeared, coming forward to stand beside Willow.

Slowly, she began once more to turn into a woman.

There was still love in her eyes as she looked at Silas – a mother's love.

'She's right, Silas. You can let it all go. This doesn't have to be you – trying to punish the world for what happened in the past. I'm so sorry that you grew up without acceptance. But no amount of power will change that. Like Willow said, you have to find a different kind of strength – the strength to forgive me, forgive Moreg, even to forgive your father.'

Silas's eyes grew dark and cold. 'I *can't*,' he spat.

Moreg Vaine stepped forward, and he turned to look at her with a sneer.

Moreg said, 'I was wrong, Silas, to give you to your father to raise. In my visions of the future, I saw you, a boy born with magic, as the leader of the Brothers of Wol – and I believed that it would bring a new era for us all, where we could finally come together and live in harmony as we once did. I didn't see how he would raise you with such hatred of all things magic until you hated even yourself. I did not see what was most likely to happen – that he wouldn't know how to nurture such a sensitive, magical child.'

Silas blinked. 'I am not sensitive.'

Then Molsa shook her head. 'Silas, I was like you –

blinded by my own need for vengeance, filled with fury over what my sister had done. But I was wrong too . . .'

'No, I was,' snapped Silas, and his face turned to stone. 'I was wrong to think that there was ever anyone I could trust. You have betrayed me, Mother – like her, like *everyone else*!'

Then he clasped the staff in both hands and banged it on the ground. It flashed with light, and there was a swirl of black smoke.

'As a lost soul, it is time you went back to Netherfell. I have summoned Umbellifer's servants to take you away,' he hissed, his eyes glittering darkly.

Willow's gaze darted to Molsa, who was staring at her son in shock.

'You didn't know I had that power, did you, Mother? Well, with the staff, there's little that is beyond my reach. I have been preparing for this moment ever since you started to question me, in case you ever betrayed me – and now you have. You brought this on YOURSELF!' he roared.

Willow looked up as a smoky darkness stirred above them. Before their eyes, the inky shapes grew into an enormous carriage travelling across the sky. Then, slithering out of the windows, came a pair of shadowy wraiths.

Willow blinked in horrified recognition. They were the servants of Umbellifer, the Queen of the Undead.

'She is one of your lost souls,' announced Silas as the wraiths descended, pointing the staff at his mother. 'Take her!'

The wraiths acted quickly. Willow and her friends stood powerless as, in a brief moment, they enveloped Molsa in swirling shadows and whisked her away. In seconds, both Molsa and the shadowy wraiths had dissipated completely.

'No! cried Moreg, distraught. Immediately, she turned to Silas and shot at him with a bolt of lightning.

But Silas was too powerful. He waved the staff at her, and the ground rose up, thick slabs of rock encasing Moreg like a cage. The witch hissed and yelled.

Silas grinned, then he turned to Willow. 'It is time we finished this,' he said to her.

He waved his staff at one of the Brothers of Wol restraining Twist, and a strange, bejewelled dagger and a glass vial appeared in the Brother's hands.

'You have a choice, Willow. You can either give me the iron half-moon or you can watch your friend die as I use her blood to make a new one.'

The Brother held the dagger to Twist's throat. The elf girl stopped moving instantly, her face pale.

Willow swallowed, but she did not hand over the iron half-moon.

It was time. She looked at Twist, then at Silas, before taking several shaky steps back. She took a breath, closed her eyes and focused.

She felt the magic rise within her, like an old friend she could greet for one last time . . .

Now.

As her hands clasped over what she had summoned, she opened her eyes.

It was as if time were standing still. Silas's empty hands grasped in front of him, coming up with air. The Brother with the dagger at Twist's throat slackened his wrist in surprise.

Because Willow stood, at last, with the elf staff in her hands.

32

Filled with Stars

'No!' cried Silas, staring in horror at Willow.

As soon as she had summoned the staff, Willow felt as she had before the Craegun granted her magic: tired, weak and drained – but determined.

As she held the elf staff, Willow could feel the magic inside it. It was a living, writhing thing. Willow swallowed. Her chest was heaving, her eyes bulging.

The iron half-moon in her other hand was drawn from her fingers in an instant, snapping back into place on the staff like a magnet. A pale light started to glow round the staff, spreading outwards, and it was shaking in her hands, as if something inside it were trying to get loose.

As Willow held on, the now intensely bright light

around her seemed to explode like a cascade of stars –
and then Willow saw it.

Magic.

It began to change from gold to green and white,
swirling all about her, taking on the shape of a girl
made from leaves and stars and flowers. Then she
heard a voice, and somehow she knew it was coming
from this girl, from *Magic.*

'We want to be *free*, Willow. Will you help us?'

'Yes!' cried Willow.

'If you hold on to the staff, and you trust us, we
can be free.'

'How?' asked Willow.

'Just hold on. Trust us.'

'I do,' she said, and the staff in her hands still
trembled as more and more magic swirled into the
girl of leaves and stars and flowers. She whirled
round Willow, glowing so brightly it was hard to see
anything but her.

But, of course, they were not alone.

At last, Silas broke through. He reached into the
blinding light and grabbed hold of the staff, trying to
tear it from Willow – but it was as if her hands were
fused to it. Then suddenly she felt something.

Magic, the magic of the staff, filling her veins. It was like when the Craegun had breathed the cool, tingling snowflakes over her body, but amplified inexplicably. It was like lightning and thunder being poured through her body, like being filled with stars or radiating sunlight.

Then, suddenly, just as the light around the elf staff was going out, Silas managed to rip the staff from Willow's hands. He shoved her out of the way so that she landed with a thud on the ground.

Silas tried to yell in triumph, but it came out as a thin croak, and he seemed to waver slightly as he attempted to focus, as if he were dizzy.

His powers were gone, Willow realised. In the moment he'd touched the staff to snatch it back, his own original magic had escaped him, channelling itself through the staff to take refuge in Willow with the rest.

He twisted the iron half-moon and pointed it at Moreg. 'I'll begin with you. The most powerful witch in Starfell!' he cried. Except he couldn't seem to aim it properly, as if the staff were suddenly too heavy or his arms too tired. He shook his head and grunted, like he was trying to pull himself together, and then aimed it at Moreg properly at last.

284

But Willow was calm. 'It won't work,' she said.

He tried to give Willow a mocking, confident sneer as he pointed the staff at Moreg, but his hands shook, and he'd turned incredibly pale. Sweat had broken out on his forehead.

'I don't feel right,' he whispered. Then he slapped his face with his free hand as if to wake himself up, and aimed the staff once more, spreading his feet as if to steady himself.

Moreg hadn't made a move to defend herself. It was as though she could sense that he was no longer a threat.

Willow stood up slowly, gingerly. She felt odd too. Really odd. Her whole body throbbed with energy that was almost too much for her to hold.

'You think that magic is this *thing*,' she told Silas, walking over and touching the staff with a finger. 'But this is nothing. Nothing at all. Just an empty shell – a bit of old metal.'

It was true. Now that the staff had stopped glowing and its light had stopped swirling, it looked dull and lifeless. Whatever had been keeping it preserved for all these years was lost, and the metal started to rust and age before their eyes.

Silas was still holding on to it as tightly as he could, but his face was wan and he looked drained, like the staff. He blinked. 'What's happening to it?'

The gold and iron half-moons fell from the staff, closely followed by the orb that had once glowed, and there was a ringing sound as the metal hit the ground. The pieces lay there, lifeless. 'The magic has left the staff,' Willow told him, feeling it radiate within her.

But, before Silas could reply, the sky suddenly turned black.

Willow looked up in confusion, and she saw the enormous, shadowy carriage that had appeared before darting across the sky once again. It came to a standstill, parking above them in mid-air. Willow frowned.

Then, as someone exited the carriage, there was a collective gasp all around.

It was the ghostly Queen of the Undead herself.

33

Silas's Last Chance

Queen Umbellifer descended from the carriage, her hair drifting in the sky above her head like ink in water. Her face was beautiful but otherworldly – and full of rage. She seemed to swell, and behind her one of her wraiths cowered like a scolded hound.

'You dare to summon my servants, to give them orders?' she hissed as she hurtled down to face Silas. In a moment, her visage was inches from his, terrifying in its rage. 'You dare to command ME? I am Umbellifer, Queen of the Undead. It is I who commands *you*.'

And then she smiled, which was just as terrifying as her rage.

'You think you wield so much power, but you forget that I have my own world; I play by my own rules.'

Silas made to cast something at her, but nothing

happened. For a moment, he looked almost frightened, and young again.

'You, Silas, are a lost soul if ever I saw one,' said Umbellifer. Then she looked at Willow. 'I will take him,' she added. Curiously, it was as if she were asking *permission.*

Willow was feeling odd, woozy from the huge amount of magic she was carrying. She shook her head. 'Silas can still change.'

He turned to her shakily. 'Change? So I can be like you? Weak and pathetic? That's what you did to me, isn't it? You made sure you took away my magic too, so I could be like you.'

She looked at him sadly. He had always hated his magic, longed to change, and yet now it was gone he couldn't stand it. 'I didn't do this to you, Silas. You did it yourself, by trying so hard to be someone else.'

There was a pause, and then a third figure came out of the carriage. It was the ghostly form of Molsa as a hare. She skittered across the sky and hovered there, watching her son as if waiting to see what would happen.

'I would rather leave than stay here like this,' Silas hissed.

'He has made his choice,' said Umbellifer.

And then, as Willow and her friends watched, the queen enveloped Silas in a shadowy mist and swept him up into her dark carriage in the sky.

The hare turned once to look back at them, lingering as she gazed down at her sister.

Moreg was biting her lip to stop it from trembling. As the two stared at one another, the hare dipped her head in a final goodbye. Then she joined Silas, Umbellifer and the wraith in the carriage, and they watched in awe as the strange shadowy shape disappeared as suddenly as it had arrived.

34

The Girl of Magic

The Brothers of Wol stared, dumbfounded, after the vanishing carriage. Many appeared lost and confused, some looked as if their Gerful chalk had worn off, and others as if perhaps they realised they had put their faith in the wrong person.

The one who had been holding on to Twist seemed to make a decision of his own, and he released her himself, unshackling her manacles.

Twist rubbed her wrists together, and Skiron, the north wind, raced round her, free at last, still grey and pale and weak but relieved.

Willow tried to smile at her friend, but she felt faint – so very faint. It was like she was looking at Twist, at everyone, through a tunnel. She staggered backwards with a wave of dizziness, and then she

tripped, and it was like she was falling in slow motion – as if time itself were moving differently.

Her family and friends raced forward to catch her, but something encircling her prevented them. A soft, shimmery golden veil had appeared around Willow, allowing them to see but not reach her. Her sisters screamed her name, trying to get to her, but they couldn't.

'What's happening?' gasped her mother.

'Willow! Please tell me you didn't bargain your life!' Essential cried, her mouth starting to tremble.

Skiron began to gust with emotion, and Twist's hair electrified all around her as she sobbed, 'No, Willow, not for me!'

Her family started to wail. But it was nothing compared to the howl that escaped Oswin.

'*Nooooooooooooooooo!*'

He was trying desperately to reach her, pushing at the strange golden force field that encircled her. '**Please, please comes back! Don' leaves me!**' he howled. He'd turned so pale he almost looked white.

Still Willow lay motionless on the ground. She wanted to shout that she was fine, that they mustn't worry, but she couldn't. Something incredibly

strange was happening to her.

Nolin Sometimes had appeared, and kept pacing up and down and peering anxiously through the misty veil that separated Willow from the rest of them. Suddenly he keeled over backwards himself, his eyes turning white. But hardly anyone noticed that because they were so distracted by what was happening to *Willow.*

There was a collective gasp.

'Is – is she beginning to glow?' breathed Twist.

'Great Starfell!' cried Moreg.

She was. Willow was glowing in the same way the elf staff once had.

The golden veil between them dissipated, and Oswin dived into Willow's arms – which opened and then hugged him tight. She sat up, her eyes squeezed shut as they embraced. Then she let him go and finally stood, opening her eyes. When she did, it was as if she had been lit from within – like she was magic itself.

Her arms and legs were so bright they looked as if they were made of lightning. Her hair rippled with stars and leaves and flowers.

'Gadzooks!' cried Nolin Sometimes from his prone

form on the ground, his eyes going from white to blue and back to white again as a memory washed over him. 'It was never an elf staff. The name was changed over the centuries, lost to time, because the elves were the first people. It is the All Staff, and its magic was taken from the Great Wisperia Tree itself – the real source of magic.'

There were gasps and murmurs from the gathered crowd.

Willow nodded, and all at once she remembered the words of the Craegun.

If you succeed, and the staff is yours, you will have a choice. Only you will be able to make it, and it must be made freely.

The time for that decision had come.

'The magic was stolen,' she said, 'and I'm going to do what should have been done long ago.'

'What's that?' asked Twist.

'Give it back.' And then Willow smiled. 'Could someone hand me my broom?'

There was a whoop of joy from Essential, Oswin and Twist as they rushed to find Whisper from inside the hairy carpetbag. They handed her the compact broom, and as Willow pulled the Elvish Reduction

293

Rings, it changed from dull, lifeless and grey to a silvery birch that began to glow once more, the cloud-dragon feathers at the end transforming from dark grey to pale blue.

Holding it again was like greeting an old friend. 'Welcome back,' she said, climbing on. Then she looked at the others and said, 'Let's go to Wisperia!'

The mood was festive and jubilant as everyone banded together, and Willow was reunited with so many of her loved ones.

Willow, of course, led the way on Whisper, with Oswin inside the green, hairy carpetbag. Her non-magical friend, Peg, had reached them, and he climbed on to Feathering with Willow's family, while the cloud dragon's partner, Thundera, carried Calamity the troll. Skadi and Lumi – who had arrived as promised – rode on Feathering's son, Floss, who was now almost fully grown, and Sprig joined them too, flying as a raven. Twist and her aunts travelled via tornado, followed by Moreg on her broomstick, the Business, with its engines that emitted orange flames. Dozens of others joined in too, on the broomsticks that the Mementons had given away freely to ensure that magical folk

across Starfell had the means to a quick getaway. Pimpernell brought up the rear on the Ambulbroom, with Nolin Sometimes on a new broom that looked like a tiny version of the Great Wisperia Tree, which he was riding along with the sea captain Holloway.

As the group entered Wisperia, the sun was beginning to set in shades of pink, orange and purple. However, as they dived beneath the canopy and came in to land at the base of the Great Wisperia Tree, the forest was still dark and grey, its colours muted. As Willow dismounted, there was a sense of people holding their breath.

She looked at the huge tree that dominated the landscape, and, as she approached, she saw a face appear in its bark. But it wasn't at all like the face she'd seen in her nightmares, the one shown to her by Walaika. She was right: this was a kindly face, old and wise, and it looked at her as if to welcome her.

As Willow stepped towards it, magic flowed beneath her feet, tiny white flowers appearing everywhere she walked, like a beautiful carpet.

She closed her eyes and held her hands out to the Great Tree. Where she touched it, the bark began to glow – a beam that grew larger and larger, and soon

they could see what looked like veins glowing inside the trunk. The bark started to change, the black spots disappearing, turning from grey to the colour of sea glass once more.

As magic poured out of Willow, it swirled beside her once more, shaping itself into the young girl it had transformed into earlier, made of leaves and stars and flowers.

The girl held out a finger to touch Willow's hair, and a thread of gold appeared. She seemed to wink, and whispered, 'Thank you.' Then she turned and slipped inside the Great Wisperia Tree.

Finally, Willow opened her eyes, and she smiled. She had returned the magic of the staff to the tree, but she still felt something familiar coursing through her veins: it was *her* magic. It had been returned.

Around her, the forest began to change. Colours intensified as the trees turned once more into every shade imaginable.

Starfell was *alive*.

It was set to become a day of celebration. Soon someone put up magical lights to illuminate the forest as the day turned to night, and people were dancing and singing.

She saw Lumi and Sprig deep in conversation, Lumi writing into Sprig's palm, great smiles across their faces.

Several Brothers of Wol had arrived, as had members of the Enchancil, and they were chatting away to some local forest-touched people.

An odd foghorn sound made them all turn to look, and Willow laughed as she could see in the distance a really strange sight that was making everyone gasp and exclaim in awe: Holloway's large copper boat was waddling through the forest on its four squat legs. Willow grinned.

Moreg came to stand beside her. 'I knew you could do it, Willow,' she said.

Willow hugged her. Then she met the witch's

eyes. 'I'm sorry about Molsa.'

Moreg looked sad for a brief moment, and then she winked. 'It's not the end, not yet. Haven't you heard? I have tea parties with the dead.'

Willow's mouth gaped. 'That one's true?'

Moreg tapped her nose, then she looked over Willow's shoulder and said, 'Ah – your family is coming.'

Willow turned to go to them, but they were racing to meet her.

Her mother and father squeezed her tightly, and it was some time before she was able to get a word in past all their questions and exclamations.

'You were so amazing, Willow!' cried Camille.

'I hope you know we are so proud of you,' said Raine.

'We always have been,' Hawthorn added.

Willow's eyes filled with tears, her heart full.

Juniper squeezed her hand. 'You know, Willow, I've often wished I could be a little bit more like you . . . the way you're always helping other people, always making friends – I find it a bit hard.'

Willow stared at her powerful older sister, who could blow things up with her mind, and felt shocked . . . Juniper wished she could be more like her? She smiled at her, feeling surprised and moved.

Behind her family, there was a bonfire going, and Willow noticed lots of other witches and wizards were helping Moreg take things from her portal pantry to prepare a feast. Soon a giant cauldron was bubbling.

Distantly, she heard Moreg say, 'Great Starfell – not sure what I did with the salt . . .'

'This is new,' her father said, touching the gold thread in Willow's hair.

Willow stroked her hair and smiled.

'So,' asked Camille excitedly, her eyes wide, 'does this mean you have some really *AMAZING* power now? I heard if Magic touches you that can happen!'

Willow's eyes sparkled. 'I've heard that too. Let's see,' she said, then she closed her eyes and raised her hand to the sky.

After a short while, there was a whooshing sound, and something came hurtling out of the sky and into Willow's palm. She opened her eyes and looked at the tiny pot of salt in her hand.

'Oh,' said Camille. 'But—?'

Isn't it just marvellous?' said Willow, grinning hugely. Then she excused herself as she went to hand Moreg the salt. She felt like dancing.

'But, Willow?' Camille called, staring after her with a confused look. 'It's the exact same power you've always had.'

Oswin looked at Camille and then harrumphed. **'Wot a cumberworld.'**

Acknowledgements

Writing the latest Starfell during the pandemic wasn't easy and, like Willow, it felt as if I'd lost the ability to do the thing I love, as I tried and failed to write this tale. Yet, thanks to the kindness and magic of others, the story came slowly to life. Chief magic-wielder being my lovely editor, Julia Sanderson, who patiently over the months helped to untangle plot threads, inspire new directions and cheer me on every step of the way as I came crawling to that finish line.

Likewise, with my wonderful agent, Helen Boyle, who is just one of the best and most fun humans around – thank you for our long chats they mean the world!

A huge thank you to everyone at HarperCollins *Children's Books* for their hard work and creativity, including Ann-Janine Murtagh, Harriet Wilson, Elorine Grant, Laure Gysemans, Alex Cowan and Louisa Sheridan – you're all stars.

A giant thank you, as ever, to the kind-hearted

genius that is Sarah Warburton. Your illustrations, as always, are objects of wonder and joy, and having you bring the world of Starfell to life will always be a life highlight.

Last but not least, a massive thank you to you, the reader, for your enthusiasm for Willow and Oswin – I can't help noticing how often he steals your affections. (I is okay wiff this, yep.) Thank you for joining them on their latest adventure and for all that you do in sharing your support for this series – it means the world.